THE BASTARD OF BRITTANY

THE WOLVES OF BRITTANY #3

VICTORIA VANE

Text copyright by the Author.

This work was made possible by special permission through the de Wolfe Pack Connected World publishing program and WolfeBane Publishing, a dba of Dragonblade Publishing. All characters, scenes, events, plots and related elements appearing in the original World of de Wolfe Pack connected series by Kathryn Le Veque Novels, Inc. remains the exclusive copyrighted and/or trademarked property of Kathryn Le Veque Novels, Inc., or the affiliates or licensors.

All characters created by the author of this novel remain the copyrighted property of the author.

DE WOLFE PACK: THE SERIES

By Alexa Aston
Rise of de Wolfe

By Amanda Mariel
Love's Legacy

By Anna Markland
Hungry Like de Wolfe

By Autumn Sands
Reflection of Love

By Barbara Devlin
Lone Wolfe: Heirs of Titus De Wolfe Book 1
The Big Bad De Wolfe: Heirs of Titus De Wolfe Book 2
Tall, Dark & De Wolfe: Heirs of Titus De Wolfe Book 3

By Cathy MacRae
The Saint

By Christy English
Dragon Fire

By Hildie McQueen
The Duke's Fiery Bride

By Kathryn Le Veque
River's End

By Lana Williams
Trusting the Wolfe

By Laura Landon
A Voice on the Wind

By Leigh Lee
Of Dreams and Desire

By Mairi Norris
Brabanter's Rose

By Marlee Meyers
The Fall of the Black Wolf

By Mary Lancaster
Vienna Wolfe

By Meara Platt
Nobody's Angel
Bhrodi's Angel
Kiss an Angel

By Mia Pride
The Lone Wolf's Lass

By Ruth Kaufman
My Enemy, My Love

By Sarah Hegger
Bad Wolfe on the Rise

By Scarlett Cole
Together Again

By Victoria Vane
Breton Wolfe Book 1
Ivar the Red Book 2
The Bastard of Brittany Book 3

By Violetta Rand
Never Cry de Wolfe

Contents

Chapter One 1
Chapter Two 9
Chapter Three 22
Chapter Four 27
Chapter Five 35
Chapter Six 47
Chapter Seven 55
Chapter Eight 68
Chapter Nine 80
Chapter Ten 106
Chapter Eleven 124
Chapter Twelve 134
Chapter Thirteen 151
Epilogue 159
Author's Note 163

Much have I fared, much have I found.

Much have I got from the gods.

– The Ballad of Vafthruthnir

CHAPTER ONE

Kingdom of Brittany
905 A.D.

"IT IS FINISHED!" Queen Oreguen declared with a satisfied smile. "Come and see it."

Stabbing her needle into her tambour frame, Gwened rose to examine her mother's handiwork. "It's lovely," Gwened murmured, stroking the silky fabric with a reverent caress. The exquisitely embroidered veil was made of ivory Byzantine silk as delicate as gossamer. The queen had embellished it with equally delicate edging of gold thread. The effect was both subtle and sublime.

"It is for you," her mother said with a nod. "You marry in less than a month and must have a suitable headdress for the wedding."

"Thank you, Mother for the beautiful gift," Gwened said.

"Try it on." The queen removed her own circlet of

gold and offered it to Gwened to replace the cloth fillet that currently held her linen veil in place. "As the Countess of Poher," the queen said, "you will wear such a coronet of gold."

As Gwened donned the headdress, her foster sister Adèle looked on in open admiration. "You are beautiful," she gushed. Smiling, she clasped both of Gwened's hands. "The day is fast approaching when we will be sisters in truth. Do you grow nervous?" she asked.

"What bride-to-be is not?" Gwened replied.

Although she was indeed nervous, excitement mixed with her anticipation. She had known Hugo of Poher for most of her life. He was young, strong, handsome, and morally upright. In sum, he was everything a woman could desire in a husband. Gwened was blessed indeed to be betrothed to such a man.

The king and queen couldn't be happier about the forthcoming nuptials. They both greatly esteemed Hugo, perhaps too much. Their adoration was a source of bitter resentment to their own son, Rudalt.

Hugo naturally excelled in nearly every endeavor—swordplay, archery, riding, and swimming. He was also an avid scholar, passing much time with the monks in the abbey libraries. Rudalt, on the other hand, occupied himself with drinking, whoring, and the lowest company. The only thing the two men had in common was a passion for hunting, the only sport in which Rudalt was Hugo's equal.

"Have you chosen a gown?" Adèle asked.

"I have bought the cloth for a new one," Gwened answered. "It is a very fine linen of kermes scarlet. I think now I must embroider the hem and cuffs with gold thread."

"I would do it for you as my wedding gift," Adèle offered, "but I fear my needlework is far inferior to yours."

"You do well enough," Gwened said. "But I am useless in the still room, aside from identifying the proper plants for dyes. I think your medicinal knowledge is far more useful than my embroidery."

"We each possess our own unique gifts," the queen remarked. "And it is for each of us to find a way to ply our particular skills for the greater good."

"Yes, Majesty," Gwened answered, wondering wryly how her embroidery could possibly benefit the kingdom of Brittany.

Oreguen was a dutiful queen, but hardly an affectionate mother. Duty always came first, and she expected her daughters to follow her example. Thankfully, it was Adèle, rather than herself, who would eventually replace Oreguen, albeit, as a duchess, rather than as a queen.

Not trusting his own son, Rudalt, to rule the entire kingdom when he passed on, King Alain had recently taken measures to divide the power. Instead of inheriting the entire kingdom, Rudalt was destined to share Brittany with his two brothers-in-law, Gormaelon, the Count of Cornouailles, who had wed the king's eldest daughter Avicia, and Hugo, Count of Poher, who would soon espouse Gwened.

Gwened had long suspected that it was the king's secret desire for Hugo to eventually wear the crown of Brittany. Although it seemed unfair that Rudalt would not inherit all of his father's kingdom, in all truth, he was not worthy of it. Perhaps if he wasn't so disagreeable, Gwened *might* have felt more compassion for her brother, but the one she truly felt sorry for was Adèle who had been betrothed to Rudalt at birth.

"The hour grows late," the queen announced, putting away her embroidery implements. "'Tis nigh time for vespers." She then looked through the window of the solar with a frown. "'Tis strange I have not heard the hunting party return. Rudalt knows how much it displeases me when he is absent at prayer time."

"Perhaps it is precisely why he does it?" Gwened suggested.

Rudalt openly defied the king and queen at every opportunity.

The queen sighed. "Indeed, he seems to take great joy in my distress, but Hugo?" she asked.

Always punctual and polite, Hugo would not be late to prayer without a good reason. Where were they?

"Perhaps they had an unsuccessful hunt and did not wish to draw attention to it?" Adèle offered.

The return of a hunting party was generally a raucous event with barking dogs and much roistering. But there would be little cause for celebration if they had failed to bring home any game.

"I will go down to the kennels and inquire," Gwened said, glad to get out of doors and escape from under her mother's thumb at least for a short while.

Removing her new veil and cornet, she quickly took them to her chamber and then darted down the narrow staircase to the great hall. Her father was there in conference with a number of his men. Rudalt and Hugo were not among them.

Following protocol, Gwened held her tongue until the king chose to acknowledge her.

"What is it child?" he asked.

"The queen wishes to know if the hunting party has returned."

"Nay." The king frowned. "I was about to send men out to search for them."

His statement was echoed by a chorus of shouts and howling dogs emanating from the inner bailey. There was nothing unusual in the cacophony of sounds, but the tone wasn't right. This was not a happy arrival. The men immediately took to their feet and bolted from the great hall with Gwened following timidly behind them.

Four men had set out early that morning but only three had returned. Rudalt dismounted first. His horse's flanks heaved as if it had been galloped to exhaustion while Hugo's hunting hounds circled aimlessly and continued to howl. Curiously, while Rudalt's face and clothing were splattered in blood, there was no trophy slung over his saddle-bow.

She noted a very large blood-covered bundle slung

over Hugo's charger, but Hugo was nowhere in sight. She stepped toward the horse, but her brother blocked her path. "Hugo?" Gwened asked, her pulse racing with alarm.

Rudalt stared down at her with bloodshot eyes and the strong scent of lambig on his breath. "I regret to inform you, dear sister, that your beloved Hugo is dead."

Gwened stared at her brother, unable to comprehend his words. "Hugo is *dead*?" she repeated in a choked whisper.

"We were attacked by Viking marauders," Rudalt declared. "Hugo was struck down before we finally drove them off." He inclined his head to the body slung over the horse. "There was nothing to be done for him."

Gwened suddenly felt the ground swelling beneath her feet. It was as if she stood on a ship in rough seas, rather than on dry land. "I cannot breathe," Gwened gasped, clutching Rudalt's arm in the fear that she might actually swoon.

"What is amiss?" Adèle had appeared, wearing a look of concern and confusion. "Where is my brother?"

"Slain by Vikings," Rudalt growled. "I must inform the king." He ruthlessly shook off Gwened's hold and pushed past the two women, bound for the keep.

Still in shock, Gwened stared after her brother. "Hugo is dead," she whispered, her voice sounding flat and wooden even to her own ears. Suddenly, Gwened's eyes began to blur and her knees quivered. It wasn't real. This couldn't be!

"Gwened?" Adèle murmured her name but Gwened couldn't seem to respond. Although she stood in front of her, Adèle's voice seemed so very far away. Gwened shut her eyes as Adèle pulled her into her arms with a great sob. "My poor brother! My poor, Gwened!"

The dogs encircled them, erupting into a howling chorus of mourning as the two young women held each other and wept.

CHAPTER TWO

A FORTNIGHT AFTER Hugo's death, Gwened still struggled with shock and disbelief. Donning her wedding veil, Gwened wandered her chamber, feeling much like a ghost of her former self. She'd wept for days on end, until there were no tears left. The entire kingdom mourned the young Count of Poher's passing, or better said, the entire kingdom, save Rudalt. His reaction to Hugo's death was strangely cold. What exactly had happened on their hunt?

Gwened struggled to puzzle it together. Her unease over the incident was compounded by inconsistencies in her brother's story. The king's men-at-arms had set out early the next morning to the river where the Vikings had landed their boat. Although Rudalt said they had come to rape and plunder, none of the nearby villages had been pillaged. And no one, save Rudalt and his men, had seen the boat.

Although the king seemed to accept their story,

Gwened's thoughts led her toward a path that she was afraid to take. She refused to voice the suspicions in her heart for fear of giving credence to the unthinkable. Surely her brother was not capable of such a heinous deed as murder! She must put this behind her. But with Hugo gone, what was left for her?

Marriage to Hugo was to have been her future. She had loved him for as long as she could remember and was certain that he also cared for her. She had fantasized about their life together for years. Her heart ached with wistfulness for what might have been.

A soft rap sounded on her chamber door, probably her maid with another supper tray that she would once more send away untouched. "Enter," Gwened commanded, surprised to see Adèle rather than Agnes, open the door.

"The queen sent me to fetch you to her solar," Adèle said.

"I have no desire to see anyone. Tell her I am ill."

"I too, mourn him, Gwened." Adèle came toward her with soft and sympathetic eyes. "But we both must accept that he is gone... and life... goes on."

"I still cannot comprehend it!" Gwened said. "Why did it have to be Hugo who was slain? Why wasn't it someone who would not be mourned? Why wasn't it Rudalt?"

The moment she said it, she wished she hadn't.

Adèle's eyes widened. "You should not say such things of your own brother."

"'Tis true, nevertheless!" Although Adèle was too kind and well-bred to say so, Gwened suspected that Adèle would not have mourned Rudalt half as much as Hugo.

"I'm sorry," Gwened said after a moment. "It was thoughtless of me. I didn't mean it."

"The queen awaits you," Adèle gently reminded her. "She will wonder why you tarry."

"Pray tell her I will come anon," Gwened answered.

Adèle turned to leave but then hesitated at the door.

"What is it?" Gwened asked.

"I heard something… something that I fear will further distress you."

"What is it?"

"Can I trust you not to betray me if I tell you?"

"Yes."

"I heard the king and queen speak of your marriage."

"My marriage? But Hugo is dead."

"They spoke of another betrothal."

"Surely you misheard!" Gwened protested. "I cannot believe they would talk so soon of another marriage!"

Adèle shook her head. "Nae, sister. I did not mishear."

"Who was it?" Gwened's mind raced. How could the king be so cruel as to consider another marriage when her betrothed was so recently laid in his grave? Even as Gwened struggled to understand the king's motives, the answer came. *Politics.* The proposed marriage was contrived to safeguard the sovereignty, if not the unity, of Brittany. Her betrothal to Hugo had been no different, but at least she had loved him.

"Alas, I did not hear the name," Adèle replied with an apologetic look. She squeezed Gwened's hands with a plaintive look. "Please do not let on that I told you any of this. I only wanted to save you the surprise."

"It is indeed a shock," Gwened said. "But thank you for telling me."

Although Gwened's heart rebelled against the thought of another marriage, she knew she was powerless to prevent it. As soon as Adèle departed,

Gwened removed her veil and golden fillet. Caressing the fabric for the last time, she locked them away in the bottom of her chest, burying her hopes and dreams with them.

⇢⇢⇢⇠⇠⇠

THE QUEEN SAT in her usual place, needle in hand and tambour resting on her lap. She looked up to acknowledge Gwened, her expression as always, cool and serene.

"You sent for me Majesty?" Gwened asked.

"Come forth child," her mother commanded, arms extended.

She offered her cheek for a kiss and then took Gwened into a brief and awkward embrace. Gwened recognized the gesture as sympathy. Her parents had never shown affection but today there was *almost* a hint of compassion in her mother's eyes.

"How do you fare?" the queen asked after releasing her.

"I am heartbroken," Gwened replied. What more was there to say?

"Hearts do not break," her mother corrected with an arched brow. "Whether we like it or not, they continue to beat until we die. At times such as this, we must remember that God's will is perfect, even if it surpasses human understanding."

"Don't you miss him?" Gwened asked, biting her lip to cease the quivering. Her mother strongly disapproved of tears or any show of emotion, for that matter.

The queen sighed. "The king fears Brittany will suffer for the loss of Hugo. Thus, he must take immediate measures to secure the future of the kingdom."

"I don't understand," Gwened said. "What has this to do with me?"

"Sit, child." The queen patted the cushion beside her. "And I will endeavor to explain."

Gwened took her place on a silk cushion beside her mother.

"Not so very long ago," the queen began, "Brittany was a land that suffered great strife. We were surrounded by wolves in the form of Norse Vikings. Their raids were constant and ruthless. Our people were brutally raped and murdered and taken into slavery. Many of my own kinsmen suffered such a fate, until your father, who was then Count of Vannes, combined forces with his chief rival for power, Judicael, Count of Poher. Together, these two great warriors drove out the marauders."

"I have heard this story many times," Gwened said. "Hugo told me that his father was slain at the battle of Questembert."

"He was," the queen said. "And his dying request was that our two great families would unite and share the throne of Brittany for perpetuity. 'Tis why Adèle was betrothed to Rudalt at such a tender age, and why you were also bound to Hugo. But with Hugo's death, the king is uneasy. He does not trust Rudalt and refuses to go to his grave without taking additional measures to safeguard the kingdom. To this end, he has spent many days in conference with his counselors. There is only one solution, Gwened. Though it may seem distasteful to you at present, you must wed the second son of Judicael of Poher."

"A *second* son?" Gwened shook her head in confusion. "But Hugo has no brothers."

"On the contrary, Judicael had *two* sons—Hugo and Mateudoi."

"I don't understand. Hugo and Gwened never spoke of a brother."

"Because Gwened doesn't know of his existence, and Hugo was sworn never to speak of him."

"Why?" Gwened asked.

For the first time in Gwened's memory, the ever-composed queen struggled for words. "Because he was… sickly."

"Sickly?" Gwened repeated. "Has he recovered?"

"Although his health is otherwise fair, Mateudoi's infirmity has no cure," the queen said. "At birth, his father commanded that he be left to die, but the Countess of Poher secretly defied his wishes and sent the babe away to be suckled by a peasant woman. When Judicael eventually learned that Mateudoi lived, he ordered him to be kept apart from his other children and sent him to the Abbey at Redon as an oblate."

"How very tragic," Gwened said. Her heart filled with sympathy for both the child and the mother who was forced to give up her babe in order to protect it. "I don't understand. Why would his father do such a thing? How could he reject his own son?"

The queen sighed. "He rejected the child because Mateudoi's body is misshapen."

"*Misshapen?* You are saying he is…malformed?"

"'Tis my understanding," the queen replied.

"Have you ever *seen* him, mother?"

"I have not, but rest assured that he is far from the monster that some have claimed."

"A m-monster?" Gwened's imagination immediately fired. What manner of deformity would create a monster? Two heads? Cloven feet? A tail? Gwened's horror was growing greater by the revelation. The man she loved was barely cold in the grave and now she was expected to wed his crippled brother? "How could you consider this marriage?"

"Regardless of his condition, he is still the son of the great Judicael," the queen replied matter-of-factly. "And he has thrived at the monastery. Hugo visited him several times and remarked how devoted his brother is to his studies. He believed that Mateudoi is destined to become an eminent scholar. It is our hope that his great learning will benefit the kingdom."

"What more do you know of him?" Gwened asked.

"Very little. I only know that he has spent his entire life at Redon Abbey."

"How old is he?" Gwened asked.

"Fourteen," the queen answered.

"*Fourteen*?" Gwened threw her head back with a

snort. "He is still a boy!"

"He is old enough to marry with the king's consent."

"But I do not want to marry him!" Gwened exclaimed tearfully. How could they even consider misshapen Mateudoi as a prospective husband?

"What you *want* is irrelevant. Mateudoi is no doubt as surprised as you are by the betrothal. He was destined for the priesthood, after all."

"But if he objects—"

"He cannot object," the queen said. "Mateudoi has been a ward of the king since his father's death. He will do as he is commanded… as will you."

"So that is it? Is it already decided? I am to marry him?"

The queen nodded. "It is decided. I know that you grieve Hugo and talk of another marriage must be abhorrent to you, but you have a duty to uphold."

"But why such haste?" Gwened asked. "Am I to have no time to grieve?"

"You have had a fortnight to do nothing else," the queen replied coldly. "Mourning will not bring Hugo back, Gwened."

It was true. Nothing would bring Hugo back, yet

she still couldn't bear the thought of marrying anyone else. Nothing could make this palatable to her. Her only hope was to delay the marriage. Perhaps, given time, she could think of someone more suitable? Her hopes, however, were dashed in the next moment.

"You will go now to meet your new betrothed," the queen commanded.

Gwened's pulse skittered in panic. "Mateudoi is *here*?"

"He arrived several hours ago to meet with the king." The queen took up her needlework. "You will find them in the council room."

Summarily dismissed, Gwened departed the queen's solar. Was there no escape? She was so dazed and distraught that she nearly collided with Adèle who was standing outside the door.

"You are to marry *Mateudoi*?" Adèle's eyes were wide with incredulity.

"The queen said you knew nothing of his existence."

Adèle flushed. "Hugo told me about him years ago, but I was sworn to secrecy. I know this distresses you, Gwened, but surely my brother is no happier about it than you are. Marriage was never to be part of his future. Is it his youth or his deformity that most concerns you?"

"Everything about this situation distresses me!" Gwened exclaimed.

"Hugo told me that Mateudoi's infirmity is not half as bad as people say. His left hand is crippled and his legs are bowed which makes walking difficult for him, but otherwise, he is quite normal. Hugo said that when he is sitting, you would barely even notice." Adele laid a hand on her arm. "I know Mateudoi is nothing like Hugo, but perhaps in time you will come to care for one another?"

"I will *never* love another!" Gwened insisted fiercely, her eyes blurring with tears she refused to shed.

"But if the king commands this, what choice have you?"

"None," Gwened whispered with morose resignation. There was no way out. "I have no choice but to make the best of it."

⟫⟩⟩⟨⟨⟪

GWENED ARRIVED IN the king's council chamber to find him surrounded by his advisors and several men wearing clerical garb.

"Ah, Gwened! Come forth," the king beckoned her with an impatient wave of his bejeweled hand.

Gwened felt the weight of a dozen stares upon her as she approached and made her obeisance. Yet she willed her gaze to remain fixed on the king. "You sent for me, your Highness?"

"Aye. I summoned you to meet you're betrothed, the newly vested Count of Poher." He inclined his head to a pale young man wearing the black robe of the Benedictines.

Was this Mateudoi? He looked nothing like Hugo, but after studying his face for a moment, she thought she detected a subtle resemblance to Adèle.

"Mateudoi, Count of Poher," the king continued, "I make known to you, Lady Gwened."

"My lady," Mateudoi's face flushed and he quickly dropped his gaze.

Taking each of them by the hand, the king joined them and solemnly pronounced, "Your nuptials will proceed in a sennight."

When Mateudoi glanced up at her again his pale blue eyes reminded her all too much of a scared rabbit. In truth, they had both been ensnared in the same trap.

CHAPTER THREE

Giske, Norway, 911 A.D.

"Great Odin, Allfather, god of gods, lord of earth and sky, giver and taker of life, please accept my humble sacrifice." Kneeling before the stone altar, Bjorn continued his supplication. "With this offering, I pray that you will either take this pain from me...or take me from this world."

With one great slash of his blade, Bjorn slit the squealing, thrashing animal's throat, then watched dispassionately as its struggles ceased and a warm stream of crimson stained the stone altar below.

Countless times he had come to this lonely spot in the woods offering a sacrifice in hope of gaining solace for his soul, but the gods still denied him the peace he sought. What more must he do to be free of this agony and guilt that continued to haunt him?

The soft crunch of footsteps on leaves followed by the snap of a twig drove him instantly to his feet. Blood still dripping from his knife, Bjorn spun to face the intruder.

"Valdrik," Bjorn glared at his half-brother. "You trespass where you are not welcome."

"My apologies for intruding." His brows arched as his gaze lit upon the bloody knife. "Perhaps my blood might satisfy Odin more than that boar's, but I am not willing to let you sacrifice it."

Bjorn wiped the blade on his leather trews and then sheathed it. "Why have you come here?"

"I thought I would find you here," Valdrik said. "When you were not at the mead hall, this seemed the most likely place. Drink?" he offered Bjorn a bladder filled with mead.

Bjorn accepted it and took a long drink, followed by another. He hadn't realized until now how thirsty he was. Or how hungry, for that matter. While the entire village feasted, he had chosen to abstain from food and drink. It was his act of penance."

"Haakon would have been five years old today," Bjorn said after a time. He took a third drink that emptied the bladder, then wiped his mouth with his hand. "I was raiding when they died. Perhaps if I had been here instead, my family would still be alive."

He felt Valdrik's hand on his shoulder. "Perhaps this needed to happen for you to accept the gods' will for you. Perhaps a whole new life awaits you away from this place."

"A *new* life?" Bjorn angrily shook off Valdrik's hand. His brother's words of consolation only ignited his fury. "What was wrong with my old life? Did my happiness so displease the gods that they felt the need to strip me of all that I loved?"

Valdrik raked a hand through his long, fair hair with a sigh. "I understand your pain, brother, but everything happens for a reason. It would have made no difference where you were. "The gods decree the day of our death. Whether you like it or not, in the end, all of our fates lie in *their* hands."

"Do we truly have no say in our destiny? Part of me wonders if it is so," Bjorn replied.

"Do not question the gods," Valdrik warned. "They may punish your disbelief."

"But *why* should I believe?" Bjorn exclaimed. "The gods do not hear my prayers." He spun and pointed to the pig's carcass. "Every month I come here and make sacrifices to Allfather in Astrid and Haakon's names, but it makes no difference! There is a great gaping hole in me that will *never* be filled!" He pounded his breast with his fist. "I *feel* nothing anymore, brother! I care about nothing!"

"Because there is nothing left for you to care about," Valdrik said. "And this place is a constant reminder of that…of them. You need a change of scenery. Leaving would do you good."

"And *where* would I go?"

"Hrolfr is planning another raid in Neustria. Ivar and I intend to go this time. Leave the farming to the thralls and come with us."

"Neustria, you say?"

"Aye. It is said there are great riches in the southern lands of Frankia, lands that have yet to be looted by anyone. Hrolfr wants to establish a base at the mouth of the River Seine. The Neustrians are poorly organized and know nothing of maritime warfare. We will use the rivers to raid further inland than others have ever ventured before. Mayhap we will settle there for a while?"

Bjorn snorted. "Ivar settle? He *lives* to raid."

"True enough." Valdrik laughed. "But there will be ample enough opportunity even for Ivar. Will you join us?"

A year ago, he would have dismissed the suggestion, but now he knew things would never be right again. Given the choice, he would rather raid and pillage and flirt with death than continue to walk around like an empty shell.

"Aye," Bjorn decided after considering his options.

Valdrik smiled. "Good! I am greatly pleased to have both of my brothers by my side! We three will depart in spring and make our fortune. If the god's smile upon us, we will return home very rich men."

Bjorn cast his gaze back up to the hanging carcass. "If you depend on the gods for their blessing, we may not return at all."

CHAPTER FOUR

Duchy of Vannes, Brittany

THE FIRE FLICKERED in the great hall, casting dancing shadows over the men's faces, making it difficult for Gwened to study their expressions. Nine counts comprised the war council, with Rudalt as the Grand Duke of Brittany, presiding at the table's head.

Gwened was the only woman present, albeit to her brother's extreme displeasure. But whether he liked it or not, he was bound to accept her position there. The king's will had declared that she, rather than Rudalt, would co-rule Poher with Mateudoi until he reached his age of majority—which left her essentially in charge of the county of Poher for another year.

"The Norse have returned to Brittany," declared Father Francis, the Abbot of Redon Abbey. "The bloodthirsty Pagans pillaged the Abbey of Saint Marcouf without mercy. Only a handful of the brothers escaped. Only under the saint's protection were they able to save the holy relics. Thanks be to God." Looking heavenward, he made the sign of the cross.

"The Duke of Burgundy is assembling a coalition army," declared Hugh of Nantes who had arrived with the priest. "He seeks the help of Brittany to deal with this threat."

"Why does an isolated attack on a Cotentin monastery have you quaking in your boots?" Duke Rudalt asked with a snort. "Brittany has not had to deal with any real Viking threat for decades."

"They will not stop at one monastery," the priest insisted. "They rejoice in defiling the house of God and do so in unspeakable ways."

"This is not isolated," Hugh said. There is a growing colony of them in the Loire that the Franks have failed to eradicate. If this new group gains a foothold, the Godless heathens will spread over the land like a plague."

"Let the Franks deal with their own problems." Rudalt dismissed their concern. "Brittany is separated from Saint Marcouf by the Cotentin peninsula. Once the Norse realize there are no riches to be plundered there, they will not tarry long. They will travel up the Seine and harry Paris instead."

"What if you are wrong?" Count Gormaelon demanded. "What if they are testing the waters now that the man who drove them from Brittany is dead?"

"Testing the waters...or testing *me*?" Duke Rudalt's gaze narrowed. "What exactly are you implying, Gormaelon?"

Gwened's gaze darted from one man to the other. The king would surely roll in his grave if he knew how much Brittany had weakened only four years after his death. Everyone knew the king had not trusted his own son to rule with autonomy, and this knowledge only weakened Rudalt's position. To make matters worse, rather than working to earn their respect and confidence, he flouted his authority, ruling as a tyrant and liked by no one but his mistress.

But now it seemed Count Gormaelon was prepared to challenge him. "I *imply* nothing. I speak openly! The Vikings are once more on our doorstep and you do nothing!" Gormaelon slammed his fist on the oaken council table with a thud. "We must join with Richard of Burgundy and drive them out!"

"And leave us vulnerable in the south?" Rudalt asked. "Damn the Franks! I am far more concerned about the Count of Poitou's designs on Vannes."

"As God's appointed ruler of this land, it is your God-ordained duty to care for and protect *His* church," Mateudoi's soft voice broke the strained silence. "By failing to act, my brother, I fear *you* will be damned."

Rudalt glowered at his young brother-in-law with a visage flooding with color, but to Gwened's surprise, Mateudoi did not cower under Rudalt's belligerent stare.

Although Mateudoi was well-read in history and had absorbed an extraordinary *theoretical* understanding of statecraft, he had never spoken a single opinion on political matters—until now. She wondered if Mateudoi fully understood the danger he had placed himself in by defying the duke. Rudalt was not a forgiving man in the best of circumstances. She was certain he would make Mateudoi pay for this humiliation.

"While I regret that I am physically unable to lead such an army," Mateudoi continued, "I am willing to lend my support to the Duke of Burgundy." He then looked to Hugh of Nantes. "I will raise men from Poher to drive these pagans from our shores."

Rudalt rose with a roar. "*I* am the Duke of Brittany! You will all do as *I* command."

Fearing blood might soon be spilled right there in the council chamber, Gwened stood. "Please! There must be another answer. Duke Rudalt has a point in that the land of Cotentin is indeed very poor. He is also right in saying there is no saving what has already been destroyed. It is indeed possible they will head toward Paris, but might it be a good idea to at least send a small contingent of men to the Duke of Burgundy?" she looked to her brother with pleading eyes. "If nothing else, we will then learn the strength of the Norse and their intentions."

Rudalt transferred his glower from Mateudoi to Gwened. "I will commit to nothing unless the Vikings become a direct threat to Brittany."

Hugh of Nantes shook his head. "By then it might well be too late."

❖

Kingdom of Frankia

STANDING ON THE hilltop, the three brothers surveyed the landscape. Thousands of corpses peppered the ground, their once-gleaming metal axes and swords now stained to the color of rust. Bjorn looked longingly past the field of the fallen to the river where their boats were moored—within sight, but ever out of reach.

"Hrolfr grossly underestimated the foe, not only did they refuse to pay tribute, they united against us!" Ivar pointed to the campfires that surrounded them for almost as far as the eye could see. "Now we are sitting on the hilltop waiting to be slaughtered like a herd of hapless sheep! By Odin's eye," Ivar exclaimed. "I wish I'd fallen in battle!"

Bjorn shared his brother's sentiments. They'd come seeking riches only to be routed and humiliated! But nothing about the expedition had gone according to plan. Their entire series of misadventures since leaving Norway had Bjorn wondering if *he* was the source of their misfortune. Did the curse the gods had placed on him now affect all those around him?

Upon landing on the coast, they'd worked their way inland, ransacking monasteries and churches along the way, but the riches were few. They then set out to pillage Paris, but the city had become well-fortified. The Frankish walls stood strong. After failing to take Paris, they'd made camp a few miles from the city where the chieftains conferred while the men paced the camp murmuring words of mutiny.

The counter-attack had come as a complete surprise. Unbeknownst to the Norse, the Franks, Neustrians, and Aquitainians had formed an alliance against them.

"Victory or Valhalla!" they had roared as they charged forth with ax and sword to meet the foe, but outmaneuvered and outmanned, the Viking chieftains had swiftly sounded a retreat. Now the remains of a once fearsome Viking army now blanketed the hilltop behind a fortification of dead bodies and animal carcasses.

"Enough of this!" Valdrik exclaimed, throwing down his empty wineskin. "The time has come to act!"

"How?" Ivar asked, his brows pulling together. "The only way to the boats is *through* the enemy camp!"

"Then we must go through it," Valdrik declared. "The Franks are so confident of victory that they will not expect an offense. We only want for an element of surprise to penetrate their lines. We have but one chance out of here. We *must* act tonight."

※

IT WAS EERILY quiet with the soft glow of the moon

painting ghostly patterns over the landscape when the vanguard led by Valdrik, stalked stealthily down the hill. Knives in hand, they moved as silently as shadows, eliminating the Frankish sentries with quiet lethality, until they'd advanced deep into the enemy encampment where fires smoldered and men slumbered.

Taking positions throughout the camp, the men raised their battle horns. At Valdrik's signal, they sounded a deafening peal, echoed by a dissonant din of shield rattling and Norse battle cries.

Like a stirred hornet's nest, the Franks surged from their tents, many fleeing into the darkness. Others, terrorized by the melee of screams and clashing steel, mistakenly took up arms against each other. Through the mass confusion and chaos, the Norsemen made a rapid advance toward their waiting boats. By the time the fiery ball of the sun cast its first rays over the land, the Norsemen were sailing back up the Seine.

CHAPTER FIVE

AFTER THE COUNCIL meeting, Gwened sought out Adèle. She found her sister-in-law working in her still room. Just as Gwened filled her empty hours with needlwork, Adèle spent her days grinding herbs, boiling roots, and pressing precious medicinal oils to aid the needs of those under her care and protection.

Gwened paused at the threshold to inhale the mixed scents of sweet herbs and pressed flowers. "I miss the smells of this place."

"And I miss you," Adèle said wistfully. "We see each other so rarely anymore."

"I wish it were not so," Gwened replied. "But I must soon go home."

Adèle instantly looked dismayed. "You are leaving already?"

"We have angered Rudalt," Gwened said. "'Twould be best to stay out of his sight for a time."

Adèle sighed. "You are probably right, but 'tis my

brother who has truly inspired his wrath. I was shocked to hear that Mateudoi stood up to him. I would never have expected it."

"Neither would I," Gwened confessed. "But I have learned that though weak in body, Mateudoi is exceedingly strong in his convictions." Gwened idly fingered the jars that sat upon the shelf. She opened one and gave it a sniff. It was lavender, a soothing scent and one of her favorites.

"Take it," Adèle said. "It is good for megrims."

"Thank you," Gwened said. She lingered still, desiring to confide in her sister-in-law but wondering how to broach the delicate subject. "Are you content in your marriage?" she finally asked.

"Content?" Adèle looked up in surprise. "I am content enough under the circumstances. Rudalt has his whores and I have my stillroom. I suppose I would say I have found peace in it."

"Peace?" Adèle's reply filled her with dismay. "So nothing has improved? I had hoped you and he would come to care for one another and that you would have children."

"As did I," Adèle said. "But there is little chance of that."

"Why? Do you believe yourself barren?"

Adèle released a bitter laugh. "I wouldn't know if I was or not. Rudalt prefers his mistress. If rumor is to be believed, the duke has spawned an entire litter of bastards. He is the same brute he has always been, but at least he stays away from me. Surely this cannot come as a great surprise. You know how it began between us."

"Then there is no hope of an heir?"

"None," Adèle responded with a snort. "I fear it is up to you and my brother to ensure the line continues."

Gwened sighed. "Then there is no hope at all for Brittany."

Adèle's gaze narrowed. "What do you mean?"

"I want a child, but Mateudoi denies me."

In the beginning, Gwened had understood Mateudoi's resentment of the heavy burden the king had placed upon his young shoulders but had believed that given time, he would become accustomed to both his role as Count of Poher and that of a husband. But six years of marriage had changed little. Mateudoi still conducted himself much as if he still resided in a cloister. He rarely ate meat, abstained from strong drink, and passed many hours each day in study and prayer. Most notably, he *never* came to her bed.

Adèle's gaze widened. "He does not come to you?"

"No. He does not." Gwened gazed at the teeming shelves. "Have you anything that might incite … desire?"

"You mean an aphrodisiac?"

"Yes," Gwened said, her face heating with a flush. "Perhaps it is the only way I will ever conceive a child."

Adèle's gaze flickered with sympathy. "We are both cursed. I am wed to a philandering beast and you to a monk." Adèle reached for a vial and handed it to Gwened. "While I have no hope of changing Rudalt, perhaps a bit of this in my brother's wine might suffice to stir his passion?"

"What is it?" Gwened asked.

"Ground Mandrake root. It is a powerful aphrodisiac. It is also believed to aid in conception."

"Thank you," Gwened said. "I wish it could have been different for both of us."

Adele replied with a sad smile, "If wishes were horses… beggars would ride."

Gwened prepared to act that very night when she and Mateudoi retired to their shared bedchamber. It was the opportunity she had waited for. Sleeping together was not their customary arrangement, but they had little choice at Vannes as the other guest rooms were all occupied by Rudalt's advisors.

"You surprised me this day,' Gwened said as she unbound and began brushing out her hair.

"Why?" Mateudoi's brows pulled together over his pale blue eyes. "Because I defended the Church?"

"Because you stood up to Rudalt," Gwened said. "Few men would dare to do such a thing." The compliment was not spoken just to please his male vanity, it was the truth.

"I do not fear him," Mateudoi said. "No weapon that is formed against thee shall prosper; This is the heritage of the servants of the Lord."

Gwened paused, brush in hand. "If this is so, how do you explain what happened to the monks of Saint Marcouf?"

"Do not pity them, Gwened. Martyrdom for Christ is a certain path to sainthood and all saints receive their due reward in Heaven."

"Is that why you support the idea of sending men

to fight? To become martyrs?"

"I do not condone killing," Mateudoi answered, "but the Church must be protected at any cost."

"What will happen when the burden sits solely upon your shoulders to protect us all?"

He looked confused. "What do you mean?"

"Brittany has no heirs. Should anything happen to Rudalt, the crown would fall to you."

"Adèle and Rudalt had yet to conceive a child and Gwened's eldest sister Avicia, wife of Count Gormaelon, had died in childbirth along with her infant son. As a grandson of the first Grand Duke of Brittany, Mateudoi was next in line to the throne.

He regarded her with a frown. "I do not want it."

In confronting Rudalt, Gwened had mistakenly believed that Mateudoi was finally ready to take up the mantle of responsibility, but now she realized he had only acted to protect the Church. He cared for nothing but the church.

"Is our marriage still so very distasteful to you?" she asked softly.

"Aye," he replied. "I never wanted to wed. Indeed, I would have done anything within my power to avoid this situation... but the king gave me no choice!"

His answer pained her. Gwened wondered if he ever felt sexual desire or if he just willfully suppressed it. She too, found no satisfaction in their marriage, but desperately desired a child. Moreover, the kingdom needed heirs. It was their duty to ensure the succession of Brittany. Although she found the idea far from appealing, Gwened was determined to persuade him.

Laying down her brush, she poured a glass of Mandrake-laced wine and went to where Mateudoi sat by the fire. "Mayhap this union is not what either of us wanted, but we could try to make the best of it, couldn't we?" She stared down at his gnarled left hand. His hands and face were the only parts of his body that he ever exposed. She laid hers on top of it. He stiffened at her touch.

He snatched his hand away. "I thought we *had* made the best of it. I have never placed any…demands…on you."

She knelt beside his chair and offered the chalice. "If you are uncomfortable, perhaps a bit of wine…"

"I am not thirsty." He shoved the cup away, splashing the wine and nearly knocking it from her hand.

With a sinking heart, Gwened stared down at the red stain on her white linen. "Please, Mateudoi… It is our *duty* to produce a child."

"The duty lies with *Rudalt* to produce heirs for Brittany."

"But I *want* a child!" Gwened answered in a choked voice.

"Then I am sorry for you. I am not my brother in *any* way, Gwened. My desire is *only* for the things of God."

"But relations between a husband and wife is not sin," Gwened protested. "The joining of bodies for procreation is *expected* in a marriage."

"Even so, scripture says that it is good for a man *not* to touch a woman. 'Tis better to set ones' affection on things above, not on things on the earth."

She stared at him in incomprehension. Why was he doing this? "You would deny me children?"

"If it was God's will, you would have conceived," he replied.

She let loose an incredulous laugh. "After only *one* coupling?"

His reply bitterly reminded her of their wedding night. After retiring to their chamber, Mateudoi had insisted that they pray together. They had spent hours on their knees until Gwened had eventually fallen asleep. On the night that followed, Mateudoi vowed to do his conjugal duty, if only to consummate the union. He came to her in total darkness with no murmured endearments, kisses, or tender caresses. After fumbling with her shift, he came over her, prodded once with a grunt, and spent his seed betwixt her legs. She wasn't certain if he had even breached her maidenhood. The experience was brief and embarrassing for both of them, and he had never repeated it.

"It is not unheard of," he answered.

Was he truly devoid of passion, or just fearful of it? Or was he perhaps afraid of creating a malformed child?

"Do I repulse you, Mateudoi?" she asked. The cruel irony of the question almost made her want to laugh.

"It is not you," he confessed with a sigh. "Marriage itself repulses me. It was designed for those who are too weak to resist carnal temptation. Perhaps it is the frailty of my body that has given strength to my spirit, but I have no taste for the temptations of the flesh."

"Have you never experienced desire...of *any* kind?"

"I have not."

She wondered at his words. She had heard rumors of men who entered the monasteries purely to fill unnatural desires. Was he one of them?

Determined to discover the truth, Gwened loosed the ribbon at her neck and let her gown slip from her shoulders. The fine linen fell with a whisper to puddle at her feet. She had never acted with such boldness before, but she was growing desperate.

"Look at me, Mateudoi, and tell me you feel nothing."

His eyes barely flickered. "I'm sorry, but you ask for what I cannot give you."

He reached to the floor and retrieved her shift. "Cover yourself, Gwened. The chamber is cold."

Mortified with shame and humiliation, Gwened snatched the garment from his hands with a stifled sob. "Not half as cold as your heart."

※》》《《※

Gwened awoke to find a sealed parchment on the pillow beside her head. Sitting up, she rubbed the sleep from her eyes and broke the wax. The handwriting was Mateudoi's and the missive was written in Latin.

She squinted at the neatly penned script, struggling to make sense of it. Although she understood the spoken language, she had never learned to read it well.

Only two phrases stood out to her—*Consummatum est* and *decreta nullitate.*

It is finished and decree of nullity? The words stunned her. What did this mean? Did Mateudoi plan to repudiate their marriage?

"Have you seen the count?" Gwened asked her maid, who had come to light the fire.

"He departed this morn with Father Francis," Agnes answered.

"Are you quite certain?" Gwened asked.

"Aye. I heard him call for his litter," Agnes said.

Why would Mateudoi have departed with the priest instead of returning to Poher with her? Did Mateudoi truly intend to appeal to the Pope for an annulment? How could he do such a thing without even discussing it with her?

Although Gwened longed to be free of the unhappy marriage, in all truth, she would not be free at all. If Mateudoi renounced the marriage, she would find herself under Rudalt's protection. Even worse, Poher would fall under the authority of her volatile and unpredictable brother—precisely what her father, the king, had tried to prevent. What to do? Should she follow him? She briefly considered it but knew the effort would be futile. There was no changing Mateudoi's mind once it was made.

"Let us leave this place, Agnes. I wish to go home."

"Now?" Agnes asked. "Should we not await milord's return?"

"No," Gwened answered. "I don't know where he has gone or when he will return…if he returns at all. I must go now before my brother gets wind of this."

"But Milord has taken the litter," Agnes protested.

"No matter, I will borrow Adele's palfrey and ride home. If Mateudoi has abandoned us, it is now up to me to rule Poher."

Agnes' eyes widened. "What of Duke Rudalt? You would defy him?"

"I will do as my father wished. I must protect Poher from Rudalt. I will defend what is mine."

CHAPTER SIX

TWO MONTHS AFTER the fateful battle that had thwarted their designs on Paris and Chartres, the Norse were entrenched along the Seine, where they could easily harry anyone who traveled the river. No one was allowed to pass without paying a hefty fine. Any who refused forfeited their vessels. This new form of piracy proved surprisingly profitable. Hrolf quickly amassed both a fortune and a small fleet.

Faced with this situation, the King of the Franks had been forced to negotiate.

"Why should we treat with them?" Ivar grumbled. "We control the mouth of the Seine and all the surrounding lands. We cripple their trade at will."

"But for how long?" Valdrik countered. "We already fight rival forces from our own race and now the Franks, Neustrians, and Aquitanians are united. Hrolfr believes we would serve ourselves best to negotiate with these Franks. Their lands are fertile and there are many among us who would be well content to take a Frankish wife and turn his hands from the sword to the plow."

"Others would rather plow the Frankish woman and move on to greener pastures," Ivar remarked.

"Not that we are finally in a position of strength, we *will* treat with them," Hrolf declared.

On the designated day, however, the Frankish forces, bedecked in full combat regalia, appeared prepared for war rather than peace. The gleaming helmets, lances, and long swords rattling against mail hauberks added a deafening cacophony to the earth-quaking thunder of five hundred sets of iron-shod horses.

The Archbishop of Reims, King Charles' chief emissary came forth to greet the Norse chieftain. "His Majesty is prepared to offer you Rouen and all lands bounded by the rivers Bresle, Epte, Avre, and Dives in exchange for the cessation of all raiding and plundering of his Majesty's kingdom," stated the king's emissary.

"But these are the very lands we already control," Hrolfr pointed out with a laugh.

"Yes, but by the terms of this treaty, they will become yours uncontested and freehold."

Hrolfr rocked back on his heels and speared the king of the Franks with his most ferocious stare. "It is not enough."

The king urged his horse forward until he looked straight down on Hrolfr, who would otherwise have dwarfed him. It was an obvious intimidation tactic. Little did he realize that one swipe of Hrolfr's great arm could land his royal Frankish arse on the ground.

"I also grant you the kingdom of Brittany," the sovereign of the Franks offered.

Hrolfr eyed him with a quizzical look. "Generous indeed to offer lands you do not possess."

The king's smile broadened. "Brittany is without a strong ruler. Since Alain's death, the kingdom is divided and contentions run high. If invaded, it will easily crumble. It is yours for the taking."

"If that is all true, why have you failed to take it?" Hrolfr asked.

"I have been occupied elsewhere," the king answered, adding with a sly smile. "And I pledge to remain occupied thusly, should your men discover an ungovernable urge to raid and plunder."

"You will not contest me for it?" Hrolfr asked, his eyes taking on an avaricious gleam.

"I will not," the king replied. "But in return for this fiefdom, I would demand a sworn oath that you and your men will henceforth secure my borders from any other invaders and serve me in any other requested capacity."

"There is one further contingency," the archbishop said. "All of your men must renounce your pagan worship and be baptized into the Holy Catholic Church of our blessed Lord."

The ranks of Norse erupted in a rumble of low curses.

The archbishop continued unaffected. "His Majesty is appointed by our God and is ruled by *Him* in all things. Any vow sworn to the King is also sworn to *He* that rules the universe. Thus, without such a pledge to God, what guarantee does His Majesty have that you will not overreach him?"

Hrolfr fingered his sword with a black look. "Do you imply that the word of a Norseman is worth less than that of a Frank?"

"I would answer that the vow of a *Christian* carries infinitely more weight than that of a pagan," the archbishop replied. "These are non-negotiable terms. Do you accept them, Norseman?"

"I must also confer with my counsel," Hrolfr replied.

By now, all of the Norse were seething with the urge to shed Frankish blood over the mass of insults piled upon them. It made little difference to Bjorn, however, he had already lost faith in his own gods. Perhaps he would have better luck offering his sacrifices to the White Christ?

Though his men were enraged, Hrolfr acted the diplomat, convincing his men to keep their eyes on the prize—lands and riches beyond their wildest desires.

When Hrolfr returned, the archbishop asked, "Are you and your men prepared to swear enduring fealty to His Majesty Charles the Third and be baptized by the Holy Ghost?"

"We are," Hrolfr replied.

"His Majesty's generosity exceeds all bounds," remarked the Marquis of Neustria. "A show of humility to one's liege lord is most befitting this occasion."

"Indeed," the priest agreed. "The recipient of such beneficence should make an appropriate gesture of obeisance to the one who bestows such great gifts."

Hrolfr's expression darkened. "What mean you by

a *show of obeisance?*"

The marquis looked to the archbishop with a sly smile. "I propose the Norseman should kiss the king's foot. Surely His Majesty deserves such a token gesture of good faith."

There could be no greater insult. It was an obvious ploy by the marquis to sabotage the negotiations, given that his Neustrian lands were being bartered.

"Sometimes is it necessary to suffer unpleasantness for greater gain," Hrolfr replied calmly. "A bit of lip service is a small price to pay—even if the lips in question must be plied to the king's foot."

"*Unpleasantness?* Valdrik erupted in a humorless laugh. "A war chieftain would never so degrade himself."

"That is true, nephew. And that's why *you* will do it."

"Me!" Valdrik looked ready to explode.

"Yes. You." Hrolfr nodded. "You have made your name as one of Odin's great warriors. Now it is time to prove yourself in statecraft."

Valdrik cursed under his breath. "I'll kiss your hairy arse first, Uncle."

"You *will* do it, Valdrik," Hrolfr insisted, steely-eyed, "and with a smile upon your face. I promise you will be well-rewarded for your sacrifice."

"And what prize awaits the man who debases himself? What price do you set on my honor? My pride?"

"A crown," Hrolfr replied blandly. "A kiss seems a small token in exchange for a kingdom, does it not?"

"I will need men, arms, and horses."

"You will have your pick of three hundred mounted warriors." Before Valdrik had time to respond, Hrolfr ushered him forward with a shove. "My kinsman, Valdrik, seeks this honor."

The king's brows came together in a frown. He dropped his foot from his stirrup. His horse shifted in impatience. The seconds lengthened into minutes as Valdrik glowered at the king's foot but made no move to comply.

"This treaty will not be concluded without a proper demonstration of goodwill," the archbishop's voice rang out. "Defiance shall be construed as a declaration of war."

Exchanging looks, Bjorn and Ivar laid hands on their swords. The Frankish forces were mounted. The Norse were on foot. The odds were not favorable.

They were ready to draw their steel when Valdrik

suddenly grasped the royal foot and jerked it upward to meet his lips. The sheer violence of his act threw the king off balance, nearly unseating him from the horse!

The lines of Frankish soldiers stood gape-mouthed while the Norsemen erupted in riotous laughter. Perhaps he hadn't adhered to the *spirit* of the decree, but no man could claim he hadn't discharged the command.

After sealing the bargain with the dubious kiss, Valdrik, his two brothers, and three hundred hardened Viking warriors set out to conquer the kingdom of Brittany.

CHAPTER SEVEN

Carhaix Castle, Poher, Brittany

"Ouch!" Gwened stared at the drop of crimson forming on the tip of her finger. Her first thought was to admire the deep red color, more vivid than anything she could ever produce from madder. Then realizing she might stain her precious white linen, she laid down her needle and sucked the droplet from her finger.

What had begun six years ago as naught but a means of filling her empty hours had become her greatest passion. The embroidered cloth now stretched the entire length of the solar. Much of it was her own family history. In her mind's eye, she had envisioned the faces of the proud men and woman who had once ruled the kingdom, and her nimble fingers had brought those images to vivid life, stitch by tiny stitch. It was a long and proud heritage that she feared would be lost forever if neither Rudalt nor Mateudoi produced an heir.

She couldn't recall the last time she'd pricked her finger, but she was growing more distracted by the day. Two months had passed with no word from Mateudoi. Where was he? Had he gone to Rome to petition the pope? She found it difficult to imagine him tolerating such a long and arduous journey. Had something happened to him?

Although he kept to himself most of the time, it was strange to be alone in the castle. What would he do once they annuled the marriage? She could easily see him returning to Redon Abbey. It was more home to him than Castle Carhaix had ever been. Perhaps he was even now at the abbey, his wife and home far from his mind? Unable to stand the uncertainty, Gwened resolved to send someone to inquire after his whereabouts. Having at least made that decision, she once more picked up her needle to resume her work.

"My lady!" Gwened's maid, Agnes entered the solar with an expression of alarm. "I bear terrible news from Vannes!"

Throwing down her tambour, Gwened instantly took to her feet. "What is it, Agnes?"

"A party of soldiers has arrived with news that an

army of Vikings has invaded Brittany!"

"Where are these men?"

"They await you in the great hall."

"Go at once to the kitchens and notify the cook we need food and drink for these men!" Gwened's thin slippers slapped the flagstones as she made haste to meet the messengers. Three men with haggard faces and bloodstained clothes turned to face her as she entered the great hall.

"You have come from Vannes?" she asked.

"Aye, milady." One of the men stepped forward, his eyes grave. "Duke Rudalt is slain and a great battle wages at Castle Quimper."

"Dear God!" Gwened gasped. "My brother is dead?"

"Aye, milady." He crossed himself. "God rest his soul."

Gwened's next thought was of her sister-in-law. "What of the Duchess Adèle?"

"Best I know, she lives, milady," the captain answered. "The moment Duke Rudalt was killed we rode on to Quimper to warn Count Gormaelon, but the Vikings were swift to follow. They laid siege to the castle."

"Then I will send men at once to Gormaelon's aid!"

The captain of the trio shook his head. "Count Gormaelon has already fallen."

"What?" Gwened clutched a hand to her throat.

"These Vikings did not set out just to plunder, my lady. These godless savages have come to conquer all of Brittany."

"Conquer?" she repeated blankly. How could this be? "What news of Lady Emma?"

"She still held the castle when we rode out but 'tis only a matter of time 'til they set it aflame. We cannot fight them, milady," the captain said. "Our men have scattered."

"Tell me everything from the beginning. I must know exactly how this came about if we are to put up any defense."

The two most powerful men in the land were dead, and many soldiers with them. The ones that remained were now without leadership. Rudalt had gravely misjudged the danger at his door and now her homeland had been overrun by a pagan army. Worse, these pagans had not come just to pillage, they had come to stay.

For decades Brittany had been free of Vikings while

they ran rampant in England and Frankia. But the Franks had finally united against them and driven them into Brittany. If Rudalt had joined the Franks, might they have been better prepared to protect their own borders? He'd been warned of the threat, but his pride had overcome caution. Brittany had never been more vulnerable. Rudalt and Gormaleon had failed to counter the threat and Mateudoi was gone.

Once she overcame her initial shock, a strange calm settled over her. "Surely there must be some way we can rid ourselves of this plague. We will pay tribute if we must," she said. "I don't care if we have to empty every coffer."

"They will only return later and demand more," the captain argued.

"They almost certainly will," she agreed. "But at least it will buy us some time. We must regroup and strengthen our defenses or we have no chance at all. I will ride to Vannes on the morrow and see for myself what havoc they have reeked. I will learn what manner of foe we face and find a way to deal with them."

<hr>

THE RIDE FROM Carhaix to Vannes was three days

under normal conditions, but pushing her horse and her men, Gwened covered the distance in two. Halting on a rise about half a mile from the castle, she surveyed the landscape. To her great surprise, there were no smoldering fires or severed heads hanging from trees—the usual aftermath of a Viking raid. There was no evidence that a siege had ever taken place. Instead, it all seemed oddly quiet. Was there some mistake?

"I do not comprehend this," Gwened remarked. "It appears...so normal."

Signaling her men-at-arms, Gwened rode onward toward the castle gate. All of her senses were on alert, but there were no damaged buildings or slaughtered animals. Was this some kind of trickery designed to lure her in? Her spine was rigid and her hands clenched the bridle reins as she urged her horse forward.

Halting at the gate, she listened for the sounds of activity from within. She caught the sound of Breton voices, the complaining bleat of sheep, and the lowing of cattle. None of this made any sense.

"Go to the gate," she commanded Guerec. "Tell them I have come to see the duchess."

A moment later, Guerec returned to her. "I am told

she is not here, milady, but you are welcome to enter the gate." He nodded to the portcullis rising behind him.

"Not here?" Adèle was gone? She noted several men standing at the gate. They wore long hair and had bearded faces. Bretons were clean-shaven.

"Where is she?" she asked, her suspicion growing as the strangers approached. Had they lied? Was the duchess also dead? Gwened fought a surge of fear.

Guerec opened his mouth to answer, but another voice replied.

"She has ridden to Quimper to treat my injured brother," one of the Vikings answered in Breton. His voice was a low, soft baritone with a peculiar lilt. "You are welcome here, Lady Gwened. You must be fatigued. 'Tis a long journey from Poher."

Gwened stared at him wondering how he spoke her tongue so well. He was dressed like the others in a woolen tunic and leather trews, but his beard was more closely trimmed than the other warriors, revealing an arrestingly handsome face. His skin was sun-bronzed, his brow was straight and smooth over large eyes with thick, dark lashes. He had darker hair than most Norsemen and the strangest golden colored eyes.

"'Tis not so far," she replied, willing herself to hide her apprehension. "I often come to visit my sister-in-law," she lied.

"Do you often travel without your husband?" he asked, eying her with a look of speculation that made her skin tingle.

"I have protection," she replied, inclining her head to her three men-at-arms.

"Do you indeed?" He regarded her men with a look of contempt.

"Is my brother within?" she asked, determined act as if she knew nothing at all.

"No," he replied, his intense golden eyes meeting hers. "But I think you already know this. I think it is the real reason you have come."

He knew! What should she do? Ride on to Quimper? Turn around and go back to Poher? Before she could decide, he laid a hand on her horse's bridle. She bit back a cry of alarm as Gueric drew his sword.

"Sheath the blade," the Norseman growled. "The lady is in no danger."

"Do as he commands, Gueric," Gwened said, knowing there was no escape. They were outnumbered and he had hold of her horse.

"Come. Let us talk," he said. "We have much to discuss." Giving her no choice, the Norseman took the reins from her hands and led her horse through the castle gate.

"Who are you?" she demanded as they entered the bailey. "And what are you doing here?"

"My name is Bjorn Vargrson," he replied. "And I am looking after things on my brother's behalf."

"On your *brother's* behalf? This castle belongs to *my* brother, Rudalt, Duke of Brittany!"

"Rudalt is no longer Duke of Brittany," he replied matter-of-factly. "You!" he called out to a young Breton boy. "Take care of the horses."

Gwened sucked in a gasp as he put his hands about her waist and he lifted her from the saddle. She glared down at him only to soon find herself looking up…way up. He stood a full head and shoulders above her. She was not a particularly small woman, but he was a very large and powerful man. She was painfully reminded of Hugo. Would this barbaric invasion ever have happened if Hugo had lived?

"Do not ever touch me again without my permission." Her body trembled with fear and outrage.

He shrugged. "How else would you have dismounted?"

"I would have managed." She silently seethed as he escorted her into the castle. This invader's civility irritated her beyond measure. Nothing about this encounter was as she'd imagined. Vikings were brutal savages who ransacked and raped. They didn't engage in polite conversation!

"I suppose you know your way around," he said.

"Of course I do," she snapped. "I grew up here."

"Then you are very fortunate. It is a fine castle." He slowly surveyed the great hall with a look of admiration. "We have nothing like it where I come from."

Gwened refused to continue this inane exchange of pleasantries. She jerked around to face him. "How much do you want?"

He cocked a dark brow.

"To go!" she clarified. "How much money must we pay you?"

"We did not come for tribute," he said. "We came to conquer."

"Do you really believe you can just march into this land and simply claim it as your own?"

His answer was blunt. "Aye. Haven't we proven as much?"

Gwened gaped. The arrogance of his answer was astounding. But it was also indisputable. They had indeed claimed her ancestral home and by all accounts would soon take Quimper, if they had not already done so. Two of the most populous and prosperous provinces had fallen at their feet with barely a fight, and Poher surely would follow. They had no defense.

"Vikings rape and plunder and return at will, but you have never settled in this land…or in any other!"

"Perhaps our *will* has changed?" he suggested with a subtle smile. "There is a colony of Danes who have settled in the south of Frankia. Their chief is named Rognvald, a brutal savage. The King of the Franks offered our kinsman lands in Neustria in exchange for an alliance against them."

"But this isn't Neustria!" she said. "Did you get lost?"

He responded with a chuckle. "No. We are not lost. Quite the contrary, I believe we have found something…something worth keeping." The look in his eyes filled her with dread. He meant what he said. They had every intention of staying.

"Tell me what happened to my brother." She would have the truth of it one way or another.

"You will know all soon enough," he replied blandly. "First, you will refresh yourself. *Then* we will talk."

THOUGH BJORN REFUSED to show it, the Countess of Poher's appearance at Vannes had caught him off guard. He'd half-expected a Breton army to show up at his door, but a woman? Could she have come as a spy? Where was her husband? Was her arrival a ploy to keep Bjorn occupied while he raised an army against Valdrik?

Her arrival, however, was a grave miscalculation on her part. His injured brother would not have to worry about any trouble from Poher if Bjorn held her hostage until Valdrik recovered. She was an inconvenience, of course, but one he had to accept. Rudalt's former mistress Gisela was already trouble enough. Thankfully, Ivar had handled her, which now left Bjorn to deal with the countess. But what to do with her? Inconvenient men were easily dispatched, but women were another matter altogether. He was reluctant to keep her locked up.

The thought of having to entertain her made him strangely uncomfortable. He wasn't used to females, let alone those of high breeding, but he resolved to treat her with all the respect due to her station.

"Bring food and wine," he commanded the servants. "We have an important guest."

CHAPTER EIGHT

Feeling unnerved and seeking security, Gwened by-passed her old bedchamber and went instead to the queen's apartments, rooms that were rarely used since the dowager's passing. Rather than moving into the queen's chambers, Adèle had opted to remain in her own, as far as possible from Rudalt's domain.

Unlike the queen before her, Adèle spent most of her time in her still room, rather than in the solar. Gwened, however, had passed most of her girlhood in this room. The rays of sun shining through the window lit up the dust motes that had taken residence, but other than the light film of dirt coating the furniture, distaffs, and spindles, the room was largely unchanged.

She took up a tambour that still held a piece of gossamer thin silk, very much like the veil the queen had embroidered for her. The stitchery, depicting vines and leaves in silver thread, was tiny and perfect, the work of the queen. Gwened wistfully traced it with her fingers. Although they were never close, Gwened felt a connection to her mother in this room. Oreguen was a strong woman, and Gwened had never been more in need of strength.

Feeling somewhat fortified, Gwened left the solar to settle her few belongings in her mother's chamber. She then called for water to bathe. Her request was answered by Adèle's personal maid, Mathilda. Gwened was elated to see a familiar face at last.

"What has happened here?" Gwened asked. "Do you know what became of the duke?"

"I do not," Mathilda answered with a shake of her head. "I only know that a messenger came bearing news of Vikings, and the duke rode out with his men to confront them. He never returned."

"How could I know nothing of it?" Gwened was astonished. "How long ago was this?"

"Not long milady, barely a fortnight. It all happened so quickly! We were not prepared. The duchess only got word of the duke's death when the entire Viking army stormed the castle gates. Fearing for our lives, she negotiated a treaty."

"What kind of treaty?"

"She let them in on the promise no one would be

harmed."

Gwened snorted. "What good is a Viking's promise?" Yet, even as she refuted their sense of honor, she recalled that there had been no evidence of violence when she'd arrived at Vannes. "They held to this vow?" Gwened asked.

"Aye, milady. Our men were disarmed but only those who resisted perished."

"And the women?" Gwened asked. "How many have been raped?"

"None have come to any harm." The maid averted her gaze. "To our shame, many of them have been all *too* willing."

Gwened digested that remark slowly. The big, brawny Norsemen with their long hair and beards were very different from the Breton men. This was likely the source of their appeal to the maidens, most of whom had never been outside of their own province.

"What can you tell me about the duchess?" Gwened was almost afraid to ask.

"Milady *seems* well enough, given the circumstances. She had little choice but to wed that savage."

"*Wed?*" Surely Gwened misheard her!

"'Tis true my lady. The Viking leader who killed

the duke demanded that she marry him. Duke Rudalt's body was in the ground less than a day before he took the duchess to wife."

Gwened's heart leaped into her throat. "He *forced* her?"

"Tis not as you think." Mathilda shook her head. "I do not believe he harmed her."

"Then where is she?" Gwened asked.

"She has ridden to Quimper. The moment she got word that he was injured in battle, she went to tend him."

"Why? Why would she tend this man?" Gwened was flummoxed. Of course they would seek her out as a healer. Adèle was very knowledgeable about medicinal herbs. But why would she help them? She could hardly comprehend her sister-in-law's actions.

"I know not, milady. But she went of her own accord. That is all I know of it."

The entire story was a great mystery! The more she learned, the more questions Gwened had. She didn't know what to think of the Norseman who presumed to play host in her brother's castle. Had he intended to harm her, he surely would have done so already. He had, thus far, treated her well enough. Hostility toward him would get her no answers, but she refused to drop her guard.

An hour later, he summoned her to supper, but Gwened took her time, refusing to look like a victim of conquest arriving in her rumpled and dirty traveling clothes. No, if she was going to assert her family's rightful position in this kingdom, she must look the part. She might only be a countess, but she would act like a queen. Rifling through her mother's trunk, she found a tunic of crimson silk along with her mother's golden coronet.

She stroked the cool, smooth metal, wondering that no one had found it yet. She would have expected them to have combed the castle for such treasures. It was another piece to the growing mystery. Gwened unbound her hair and proudly donned the ancestral crown worn by the queens of Brittany. Modesty required her to also don a veil, but didn't modesty imply submission? Refusing to appear diffident, she eschewed the veil.

The Viking would recognize the worth of the queen's golden headdress at sight. If she wore it, would he snatch it from her head? She would soon know exactly what manner of man she dealt with.

ACTING AS VALDRIK'S seneschal, Bjorn sat at the head of the high table. With its tapestry laden walls and great hall with two roaring fireplaces, the four-story castle of the Breton dukes was grander than the longhouses of the richest Jarls. As the bastard son of a Norse chieftain's concubine, Bjorn had never in his wildest dreams imagined commanding such a position, but Valdrik had promised riches to both of his brothers. The only thing missing from this great victory was the knowledge that Astrid would not share in his new prosperity.

Determined to push her from his thoughts, Bjorn took a long drink of lambig, a hard cider, highly favored by the Bretons. It was a strong and unfamiliar drink to the Norse, who favored mead, but if this land was to become his new home, Bjorn was determined to adopt some of its customs.

He was surrounded by his men, a few of the former duke's retainers, as well as a handful of the Breton women, who to his men's delight, had chosen to ally themselves with the Norse. The hall was filled with food, drink, and the occasional bark of laughter.

Although his men still wore their weapons, the wariness and mistrust were gradually beginning to ease between the victors and the vanquished.

Looking over the great hall, Bjorn wondered how soon his men would begin to settle down and marry Breton women. By the look of things, it would not be long. He wondered how his brother fared with his new wife. When he'd left them at Quimper, Valdrik was in the capable care of his duchess. Valdrik had responded quickly to her treatment. His wound had improved and his fever had abated. Her actions were not those of a hostile captive, but those of a caring wife. Though Bjorn had initially suspected her motives, she had proven herself trustworthy.

Did she love him? Though he would deny it to his dying breath, Valdrik was enthralled with his Breton duchess. Bjorn had never seen him look at a woman the way he looked at her. It was almost as if she'd bewitched him.

When he'd announced his intention to marry, Valdrik had made it clear that he also expected both Bjorn and Ivar to wed Breton noblewomen, claiming it was necessary in order to keep this land they'd claimed.

"Not me," Bjorn had replied. "I will serve you in

any capacity you ask, but I will never take another wife." Following Astrid's death, Bjorn had avoided women…until now.

Where was the countess? He was growing impatient. He'd sent a servant for her nearly an hour ago. Bjorn drained his cup and was prepared to fetch her personally when he spotted her at the base of the stairs. She wore a gown of crimson silk with a golden circlet over her waves of loosely flowing dark hair. With chin held high, she entered the hall.

Their gazes met. He read defiance in her eyes, but there was also a hint of fear that she failed to conceal. She was a curious mixture of pride, poise, and defiance that stirred something inside him. He inclined his head to the vacant seat to his right. His gaze transfixed on her as she moved across the room.

"You have come at last," he remarked with a strong hint of sarcasm.

"I only came at all because you promised to tell me what happened to my brother," she said.

"Eat," he urged, waving to her trencher. "And then we will talk."

"I'm not hungry."

"Very well." He poured her a cup of cider. "I will

answer your questions if you answer mine. We will start with your husband. Where is he?"

"I don't know," she answered, gaze averted.

"I think you lie," he said.

"I do not lie!" she declared angrily. "He had some business with the Church." She then countered with a question. "What happened to my brother, the duke?"

"Duke Rudalt ventured his title and lands in hand-to-hand combat against my brother Valdrik. He lost the fight, and Valdrik came here to claim the spoils."

"The spoils included the duchess?"

"She was part of the bargain," Bjorn answered with a shrug. "So Valdrik took her to wife. When does your husband return to Poher?"

"I don't know. I expected him some time ago."

"What business did he have with the church?" he asked.

"'Twas some legal matter," she replied. "Perhaps it is already settled and he has returned to Poher."

He studied her for a long moment. She was being far too vague. She was hiding something. "Does your husband often leave you alone?"

"I have my men-at-arms," she reminded him.

Bjorn leaned back and studied her. She appeared

unusually calm for a woman who feared her husband's death. What manner of husband was he? Clearly, there was no great love between them. He could only guess that it was an arranged marriage. Bjorn counted himself fortunate to have been low born. It had kept him from such a loveless union.

"Why did you really come here?" he asked.

"I needed to see for myself if it was true that you had taken Vannes. What is your price to leave us in peace?"

"I told you, there is no negotiation. We will not be leaving."

"Then what are your intentions?"

"Our intentions?" He cocked a brow and considered how to answer her.

"You have taken Vannes and Cornouailles. Is Poher next?"

"Aye," he replied. "Your arrival saved us much trouble."

"What do you mean?" Her eyes widened. "Do you intend to keep me here? As a prisoner?"

"As a *guest*," he corrected. "You will have the freedom to move about as you please, so long as you do not abuse my trust."

"But I cannot leave?"

"Nay," he replied. "You will stay under my protection until your husband swears his fealty to Valdrik."

"What if Mateudoi refuses your demands?"

"He would be wise to consider his actions carefully," he replied. "Our men wish to settle and prosper. We intend to live peaceably, if possible, but we will fight to keep what we have claimed. Any who resist will do so at their peril."

"Like Count Gormaelon?" she suggested.

"He chose to fight." Bjorn shrugged. "Now he is dead."

"I wish to retire now," she suddenly said.

He replied with a nod. "Do as you please."

She rose stiffly and departed. She had entered the enemy camp virtually alone and defenseless, but still managed to conduct herself with the haughtiness of a queen.

After the countess retired, Bjorn stayed in the great hall drinking, recounting tall tales and exchanging good-humored insults with his men until most of them lie sprawled around the great hall snoring. Bjorn, however, had no desire to seek his bed. Instead, he sat by the fire alone with his thoughts—but those thoughts kept straying back to the Breton countess.

Everything he learned about her only stirred his curiosity to know more. There was no denying her regal beauty, with her slim figure and delicate features, but there was also steel in her spine and ice in her eyes. A woman like that challenged a man, made him wonder what it would take to soften the steel and melt the ice.

Recognition of his desire flooded him with guilt. Although his wife was long dead, he still remained loyal. Until he could forgive himself for her death, he would not betray his vows to her. But thus far, the gods had been deaf to those prayers.

CHAPTER NINE

GWENED RETURNED TO the queen's chambers feeling overwhelmed and dismayed. Her conversation with Bjorn had been much like a game of chess, each of them taking turns asking and answering questions while revealing as little as possible about themselves. Curiously, she had sought only the facts, while some of his questions seemed far too personal. Why did he care if Mateudoi frequently left her alone?

The only thing she knew for certain was that she was now a prisoner. How long before Mateudoi learned of it? And what would he do? She could hardly depend on him to ride to her rescue. Would he seek aid from the Franks? Who else could he turn to? But if what Bjorn said was true, the Franks were the very reason for this invasion!

Restless and agitated, she paced the chamber. She wondered when Adèle would return to Vannes. She still couldn't comprehend what had compelled her to help Valdrik. Why hadn't she just let him die?

Even as she questioned Adèle's behavior, she pondered her own reaction to Valdrik's brother, Bjorn. Although she passionately wanted to despise him, he'd provided little fuel to her fire. He hardly seemed like the bloodthirsty beast she'd imagined, and no one seemed the worse off for his being here. Bjorn was calm, polite, and impossible to read. But far worse was her disconcerting physical reaction to him. His rugged good looks, deep voice, and strangely arresting eyes were agitating.

Mathilda soon arrived to help her undress. "You will be sleeping here in the queen's chamber?"

"Aye," Gwened said. "I feel more secure here."

"You should know that *he* sleeps nearby in the duke's bedchamber."

"Oh." Gwened swallowed hard, wondering if she'd made a poor choice. "Should I fear him? What do *you* think of these Norsemen?"

Mathilda paused, boar's bristle brush in hand. "I do not trust them. Nor do I like that they are here, but milady Adèle suffered far worse under Duke Rudalt."

The maid's response came as no great surprise. "My brother was a brute," Gwened said. Rudalt had treated his wife abominably from the very night of their wedding. "Are you saying this Valdrik treats her with respect?"

"More like a man smitten," the maid replied with a snort. "I would not presume to guess what he thinks or feels, but anyone can see how he reacts to her."

Gwened spun around to face her. "And what of Adèle? How does she react to him?"

"At first, she only cooperated out of fear and the desire to prevent bloodshed, but I think 'tis much more than that now."

Gwened was aghast. "You think she *cares* for him?"

The maid shrugged. "I do not know my lady's heart, but when she heard of his injury, she went immediately to Quimper."

Gwened sighed as Mathilda began stroking her hair with the brush. "I wish she would return. There is so much I don't understand."

After Mathilda departed, Gwened barricaded the door with a chair. Although he had given her no reason to fear, caution prevailed. It would hardly keep him out if he truly wanted to enter her chamber, but at least it gave her a small measure of peace.

For the next two days, Gwened avoided the Vikings altogether, taking her meals in her chamber and busying herself with tidying the solar. If she was going to be a hostage, she decided she might as well keep herself occupied.

Hoping to fill her hours with needlework, she searched for supplies. There were several distaffs, spindles, tambours, and needles, but she was dismayed to find little embroidery thread. This would not do at all! Although she probably could have found a servant to procure her some spun thread, they were unlikely to have any in the colors she sought.

Gwened stared at the basket of combed wool with a sigh. She could spin it herself, but it would take her many days just to make the thread, let alone dye it. Nevertheless, the more she thought about it, the more Gwened longed to escape the castle, if only for a few hours. Bjorn had promised her the freedom of the bailey; might he also allow her to go outside its walls to gather lichens for dye?

Taking up a basket, she descended to the great hall, only to find servants cleaning up the aftermath of breakfast. "Where is…Bjorn?" Gwened asked, refusing to call him by any other title than the name he'd provided.

"Milord just left a short time ago intent on hunting," one of the servants replied.

"Thank you." Gwened hurried from the great hall in hope of catching him before he departed. She found him with a group of his men, girded with knives and spears, but with no dogs or horses. What manner of hunt was this?

He suddenly looked in her direction, his brow cocked. "Countess? Do you intend to join us for the hunt?"

The curious looks his men exchanged told her it was a joke.

"I do not hunt," she replied. "At least not anything that moves."

His brows furrowed in a silent question.

"I only hunt lichens," she explained, raising her basket.

"Lichens?" his mouth twisted. "Is this some Breton delicacy?"

His look of revulsion almost made her laugh.

"We do not *eat* them," she explained. "We use

them for dye. Your tunic is a beautiful color," she remarked with reluctant admiration. "That shade of blue is hard to achieve from woad. Do you know what kind of dye was used?"

He glanced down at his tunic with a shrug. "I am partial to this color, but I know naught of lichens and dyes."

"I do. It's one of my chief interests," she said. "I dye my own wool for my needlework. Which is why I sought you. I would very much like to go to the forest to gather dyestuffs."

His brows met in a scowl. "You cannot go alone."

"Then send a servant with me," she suggested. "I won't go far."

"How can I know this isn't a ruse to escape?"

"I suppose you will just have to trust me."

"Not good enough," he replied. He then turned to his men and murmured a remark in Norse. With snorts and guffaws, they dispersed.

"What did you tell them that was so funny?" she asked.

His glower lingered. "I told them the hunt is off and that I go instead to gather lichens."

"*You* are going with me? Why not send one of your

men?"

"I would trust any of them with my own life, but I don't trust them with yours."

"I don't understand."

"My men are used to raiding and taking what they want. I mistrust how they look at you."

His meaning made her shiver. "But *you* do not take whatever you desire?"

"I did at one time," he confessed. "But this is different. We did not come here to raid. We came to stay. If we are to succeed, my brothers and I must set the example for our men. Let us go now."

They set out on foot from the castle with Gwened struggling to keep up with the Norseman's long, impatient strides. He clearly had no liking for the task, but at least he'd obliged her request.

"Perhaps you could hunt while I collect the dyestuffs?" she suggested.

He considered the idea. "Do you give me your word that you will not run off?"

"I promise," she said. "Besides, I could hardly get very far on foot."

"True enough," he agreed. "Then you will stay here by the river and I will hunt."

He laid both of his very large hands on her shoulders with a dire look. "Do not betray my trust or you will greatly regret it."

With knife in hand, the Viking ventured into the forest while Gwened scoured the boulders and trees by the river.

Scraping the lichens was both tedious and dirty work but she didn't mind. She enjoyed dying her own wool and experimenting with colors. It had taken years of trial and error, but she had developed her own well-guarded recipes for vibrant colors. Oakmoss produced lovely lilac hues, letharia yielded vibrant yellow. Evernia could be used to achieve deep burgundy.

Spotting a fallen tree, Gwened headed toward it. Dead trees were often a treasure trove of lichen. Approaching the tree, Gwened halted at a sudden rustling of leaves. Had she disturbed a sleeping deer? Hoping to get a glimpse of it, she ventured slowly forward, only to halt again at the sound of snorting.

Gwened stifled a gasp. It wasn't a sleeping deer that she'd disturbed, but a den of wild boar! Her pulse pounded as two large, hairy animals emerged from the shadows of the downed tree. Snouts in the air, they faced her. Fearful of attack, she backed slowly away while her gaze darted about for anything with which to defend herself.

With tails and hackles raised, the pair took a step toward her.

Her heart pounded heavily against her chest. The first boar, a male, snorted and growled at her, but just as the animal prepared to charge, Bjorn leaped out of the tree line with a roar. The startled boar halted in its tracks, then spun around to face Bjorn. For a few seconds, they stared each other down. Just as it seemed the animal might retreat, the second boar advanced.

Gwened shrieked a warning but it came too late. With its head lowered to attack, the boar charged Bjorn. She wanted to run, but her feet were rooted to the spot. Gwened shut her eyes in terror, but the sounds of the struggle still filled her ears.

In the end, the boar's razor-sharp tusks were no match for Bjorn's skill with his blade. Knifed through the chest, the pig released an earsplitting squeal that put its mate to flight. Gwened breathed a sigh of relief but the wounded animal refused to give up the fight. Bjorn spun back to the thrashing boar, but rather than delivering the death blow, he proceeded to remove his woolen tunic and shirt. He then went about shredding the linen into strips that he braided into a makeshift rope that he tied around the pig's back legs.

"What are you doing?" she asked in growing confusion.

Ignoring her question, he suspended the animal upside down from a sturdy, low-lying tree limb. Dropping to his knees and looking heavenward, he murmured a stream of words she didn't comprehend, then sliced the animal's throat. Gwened watched in horror as a river of blood flowed from its body to create a crimson puddle on the ground. She shuddered in revulsion as he dipped his fingers in the blood and then wiped it down his face and across his bare chest.

Having seen animals bled many times after a hunt, Gwened recognized that he was not preparing the animal to eat but performing some kind of unholy sacrifice. Unable to watch his pagan sacrilege, she turned her back and headed toward the river.

Sitting atop a boulder, Gwened stared into the flowing water pondering the turn of events that had placed her homeland, and even her very life, in this heathen's hands. Bjorn's actions confused and frightened her. She'd begun to think of him as a man like any other, but his actions revealed a hidden thirst for blood. How long would it be before he returned to the violent nature he'd concealed so well?

After a few minutes, she startled at the crunch of footsteps. Barely looking in her direction, he squatted down by the water and began washing.

"Is this a common Norse ritual to bathe oneself in animal's blood?" she asked.

"It is *my* ritual," he replied. "I made a vow long ago that every boar I kill will be an offering to the gods."

"Why do you make such an offering?" she asked.

"My reasons are personal," he replied tersely.

As he cleaned himself, she couldn't help taking in the exposed parts of his body. She knew she should look away but found herself mesmerized. Although she hadn't seen many half-naked men, she still recognized that he was a superior specimen. He was a veritable sculpture of muscle and sinew that she admired as one would admire anything so beautifully made.

"Is this blood sacrifice limited to animals, or should I fear for my own life?" she asked.

"I only offer the blood of boars." He rose and wiped his face and chest on his tunic. "Your blood is quite safe, Countess."

"You are still covered with it," she remarked. Although his upper body was now clean, his leather-encased thighs were heavily stained.

His gaze dropped down to his trews. "I will deal with it when I return to the castle."

It was only then that Gwened realized it wasn't the boar's blood, but his own. Although the victor of the encounter, Bjorn had *not* emerged unscathed.

"You are injured!" Gwened cried.

"'Tis nothing," Bjorn declared gruffly.

"Let me see it!" Gwened insisted. "You came to my aid, at least let me clean it for you. Such wounds can be perilous if left untreated."

"It will wait."

"At least let me staunch the bleeding," she insisted. "Is there anything left of your shirt?"

"Maybe the sleeves," he mumbled.

Gwened raced back to the place of sacrifice. Ignoring the dead animal, she scoured the ground for the remains of his torn shirt. Returning to him, she mimicked his earlier actions, shredded the cloth and tied it tightly around his upper thigh.

"Come, let us return now," she urged. "I have had my fill of lichen hunting, and this needs proper attention."

Although he refused her help, Bjorn's gait became increasingly unsteady as they trekked back to the castle. By the time they reached the gates, he was staggering.

"I need help!" Gwened called out to his men. "We were attacked by a boar."

Ignoring his protests, his men carried Bjorn up to the duke's bedchamber while Gwened ordered hot water to bathe the wound. After commanding the servants, she went directly to Adèle's still room in search of healing herbs.

Entering the small room, Gwened was nearly overwhelmed by the teeming shelves. She stared blankly at the neatly labeled jars of dried herbs, ground roots, and pressed flowers, trying to recall what items might best aid his wound. Adèle was a gifted herbalist and healer, not Gwened. Why had she never paid greater attention? Her gaze rested upon a jar labeled yarrow. She knew yarrow was oft used for bleeding. She grabbed the jar along with mandragora for pain.

※

BJORN'S INJURY WAS far worse than he had let on, but he refused to let the countess see any weakness. If she'd realized the extent of his injuries, she might have run off and he could never have caught her. But by the time they reached the castle, he was completely drained of strength. His men carried him to the duke's bedchamber where he struggled to remove his trews. The blood saturated leather stuck to his skin.

"We'll need to cut them off," his captain, Lars declared.

"Then do it!" Bjorn ordered with a curse.

The gashes made by the boar's tusks were long and deep, but at least the bleeding had slowed, now only leaking when he moved. He was lying completely naked on the bed when the countess arrived. She froze on the threshold, her pupils widening and her face flushing a deep shade of red.

"It needs cleaning," Lars said.

"The countess will do it," Bjorn replied. "You may go now. Come," he beckoned her. "As you see, I am ready to be tended. Have you medicine?" he asked.

"Aye," she replied, quickly averting her gaze. "I have yarrow for a poultice and lambig to ease the pain and aid sleep."

"Lambig I will take," he said. "I am thirsty."

"Mayhap 'twould be best if your men were to assist ..."

"Do you go back on your offer to tend me?" he asked. She was a married woman. Why did she act like a maid? "Come now, countess," he chided. "You are wed. Surely you have seen a naked man before."

She licked her lips. "Never in full light of day."

She came slowly toward him, offering a bed linen. "Perhaps you could cover up that which is not injured?"

He humored her request. With a groan against the pain, he pulled himself to a sitting position and covered his lower body with the sheet, leaving only his right leg exposed. The wound, however, was only inches from his groin. He thanked the gods that the boar hadn't aimed his tusks any higher.

She poured some liquid into a cup mixed it with some powder and offered it to him. "You might wish to drink this before I touch the wound.

"What is it?" he asked with a sniff.

"Something to ease the pain." The liquid sloshed against the sides of the cup as she extended it to him.

"I make you nervous?"

She did not answer, but her gaze flickered to his as he rested his hand on top of hers.

"I promise I will not bite you," he said. "Even if I had the will, I haven't the strength." Accepting the cup, he drained it in a few long swallows. He watched her intently as she prepared a poultice for his wounds.

When she finished with the poultice, she knelt beside the bed and dipped a piece of linen into a bowl of steaming water. Her touch was uncertain as she gently began to wipe away the blood.

Bjorn's body tensed, but it wasn't as much from pain as from awareness of her touch on his bare skin. It had been a very long time since he'd known a woman's caress. Her kneeling position, made it even worse, filling his head with lascivious thoughts.

"I must clean the wound well," she said. "But I will try not to hurt you."

He laughed. "Norsemen do not fear pain. It reminds us that we are alive."

"By the look of this leg, you must feel very much...*alive*," she remarked dryly.

He bit back a hiss of pain as she began prodding the gash, and then mumbled a curse as she pressed the cloth deep into the wounds. After several excruciating minutes, she stopped. He dropped his head back with a groan of relief.

"Tis as clean as I can get it," she said. "But I fear 'twill not heal easily unless the flesh is sewn back together. I have some embroidery needles and thread in the solar. I could get them and stitch it for you," she offered.

"Poking and prodding the holes in my body wasn't enough for you?" he asked with a laugh. "Now you're going to stick me with needles?"

"I thought you said Norsemen relished pain?"

"I said I don't fear it, but I never said I *love* it. I suspect you are relishing this opportunity to torment me."

"Then you would be wrong," she said. "I do not take joy in anyone's pain, be them friend or foe."

Although she still regarded him as her enemy, her actions indeed matched her words. She had tended him with gentleness and compassion. There was much about this Breton woman to admire besides her physical beauty. He hadn't experienced this kind of interest, or any interest in a woman for that matter, in a very long time.

His gaze sought hers. "I do not wish to be your foe, Countess."

"But how can it be any other way?" she asked softly.

"The duchess made peace with my brother," he suggested.

"I suspect she was given no choice." Her gaze abruptly broke from his. "I will return anon." She laid down her cloth and poured him another cup of her special pain potion before departing.

Through bleary eyes, Bjorn watched her go. The medicine was finally beginning to work. His eyes were growing increasingly heavy as the seconds passed, but his body was light as air. His mind drifted as he let his head drop back onto the feather-stuffed pillow. He felt as if he were floating on a cloud and looking down upon himself. Higher and higher he continued to rise, into the clouds, and toward a ball of blinding light.

"Bjorn, son of Vargr," an unearthly feminine voice spoke from the light. "I have heard your prayers."

"Who are you?" Bjorn asked, heart racing.

"I am the mother of all and the spinner of fates."

"You are Frigg?" Was this really the goddess or merely a figment of his imagination?

"Your pain has been my pain," she said. "I, too, lost a beloved son."

His heart raced. "Then you will return my family to me?"

"Sadly, I cannot," she replied. "But take comfort that Astrid and your son live with the gods."

"If you will not return my family to me, please let me join them."

"That is not your decision," she replied. "Your time has not come."

"But you said you heard my prayers!" Bjorn protested.

"I have indeed," she replied. "You have been forgiven."

"What do you mean?" he asked.

"I have released you from the guilt that binds you. Isn't this what you sought with your sacrifices? And now I offer you a greater gift. The wound in your heart will be healed by the one who is destined to be your life mate."

"My life mate? I had a life mate and you took her from me!" Bjorn cried. "I want no other wife. I want Astrid back!"

The goddess' voice became louder, booming in his ears and causing the clouds to rumble. "You presume to know more than the one who weaves the threads of fate?" she angrily demanded. "When the gods answer, 'tis advised to accept their decisions with humility and gratitude."

"Forgive me, Frigg. I meant no disrespect."

The goddess continued in a milder voice, "Your son will be a king and the conqueror of many lands."

"Kings and conquerors? This is Valdrik's destiny, not mine!"

His body suddenly seized as if struck by lightning. He could neither move nor breathe. His ears still rang with Frigg's angry voice. "You have been freed, Bjorn. Reject my gift and I will forever be deaf to your prayers."

Bjorn jolted awake at a sudden stinging sensation in his thigh. He opened his eyes to a woman kneeling on the floor, head bent over his injured thigh. His muddled mind fixed immediately upon the crown she wore on her head. Strange, he'd always imagined the messenger goddess' hair would be gold. "Fulla?"

"What did you say?" It was the countess who looked up at him with her soft green eyes and a threaded needle in hand.

"Nothing," he mumbled, feeling confused and foolish. It had felt so real to him. Was it but a fantasy brought on by the drugged drink?

"I am sorry if I hurt you," she said. "I had hoped

your sleep would be so deep that you wouldn't feel it."

"Feel?" He'd hardly noticed the needle, but lightning had jolted him to the core.

Squeezing his torn flesh together, she pierced his skin a second time and drew the suture through. He watched her work with a sense of fascinated detachment. Her stitches were small and neat and evenly spaced. "You have had much practice at this?"

"Not exactly. I have embroidered for many years but 'tis the first wound I have sewn."

"You do it well. I would like to see your other needlework." He added with a smirk, "I am in need of a new shirt."

Her brows rose haughtily. "And you expect *me* to make it for you?"

"*Expect?*" He shook his head. "I expect nothing, but I would be grateful if 'twere made by your hand."

"Who made your other shirts?" she asked.

"My wife sewed most of them."

Her gaze jerked up from her work. "Your *wife*?"

"Aye, but her stitchery was not as good as yours."

Her hand paused. "*Was* not?"

"She is dead," he answered flatly.

"I'm sorry."

Her expression compelled him to elaborate. "My wife, son, and an unborn child. I lost all of them one summer while I was raiding."

"All of them?" Her eyes widened. "How?"

"There was a fire. I don't know the details. They had been dead for weeks when I returned."

"I also lost someone I loved… the man I was betrothed to."

He read pain her eyes. "A man you loved?"

"Aye." She averted her gaze. "He was killed by a band of Viking raiders."

He digested that slowly. It did much to explain her animosity and fear. "I come from a harsh place where only the strong survive. The winters are long and hard and most of our stores are depleted by spring. Raiding is a means of surviving until the harvest. It is a way of life for us."

"Do you deny that Norsemen take great delight in bloodshed?"

"I do not deny it. Many do."

"But not you?" she asked.

"I did at one time," he confessed. "I have killed many men, Countess, but I have never harmed a woman." Somehow it was important that she knew that. He wanted her respect, but not her fear. "Do you believe me?"

She stared back at him as if struggling with her answer. "I suppose I have to believe you. I have seen no evidence of violence to women here, but that doesn't mean I trust you."

"Do you trust any man?" he asked.

"I do not."

"Not even your husband?"

"No." She made no effort to deny it.

"You do not love him."

She shook her head. "I never did."

"Yet, you married him?"

"It wasn't by choice. Our marriage was arranged by the king after Hugo was murdered."

"How long has it been since Hugo was killed?"

"Six years," she replied. "But I remember it as if 'twere yesterday. I think the pain will never fade."

"It does not lessen," he said. "I lost my family three years ago. I will never be the same." Yet, as he watched her work, Frigg's words echoed inside his head. *The wound in your heart will be healed by the one destined to be your life mate.*

As Bjorn lay naked in the bed, Gwened could barely keep her mind focused on her task. His thighs were thick with muscle and covered with dark hair that prickled her skin as she worked. Although his more intimate parts were now covered, *that* portion of his body was at eye level every time she glanced up. The size and shape of him were clearly defined. Were most men thus proportioned? Mateudoi surely was not!

The sight of Bjorn sprawled out in all of his masculine glory stirred something strange and unfamiliar deep inside her, a feeling that was impossible to ignore. Her face flushed with awareness of her wayward thoughts. Virtuous women were not supposed to have such lurid imaginings. Nevertheless, she had oft wondered what her wedding night would have been like had she not wed Mateudoi. Would she have found any satisfaction in the marriage bed had Hugo lived?

She couldn't help wondering how this man had felt about his dead wife. Were they happy together? "Did you love her?" the question somehow slipped from her lips.

"I did," he answered.

"Yours was not an arranged marriage, then?"

"Nay." He laughed, a full-throated chuckle. "Her father had much higher aspirations. He had hoped for a union with Valdrik."

"If you are brothers, why would her father object to you? He would still achieve an alliance with your family."

"He objected because I am a bastard. My mother was a concubine, which means I had no inheritance. Nevertheless, Astrid still chose me."

"She was given a choice? She was allowed to marry for love?"

"Why do you seem so surprised?" A hint of a smirk hovered over his lips. "Do you think Norse savages are *incapable* of love?"

"I never thought of it at all," she snapped.

Gwened cut the thread and then smeared the wound with a thick and sticky paste comprised of yarrow and honey. "My sister-in-law is the true healer, but I hope this will prevent putrefaction. You must apply this to the wound daily."

She froze when he laid his large callused hand on hers. "Thank you."

"It needed tending."

Gwened swiftly pulled her hand away and then proceeded to collect her sewing implements. His mere touch made her tremble. Why did she have such a strong reaction to him? "'Twould be best if you do not move about excessively," she advised, willing her voice to remain cool and steady.

He snorted with contempt. "I will not stay abed, if that's what you mean."

"I didn't expect you would, but please be mindful of it and tell me right away if it reddens or becomes swollen."

Gwened left his chamber feeling angry and confused. The world suddenly seemed so unfair. She was a devout Christian and a dutiful daughter. Why had God forced her into a loveless and childless marriage? She envied this Norseman's wife. Even his heathen bride had known both a husband's devotion and the joy of motherhood. She was overwhelmed with a sudden sense of desolation.

She felt robbed.

CHAPTER TEN

Avoiding Bjorn, Gwened confined herself to the solar where she applied herself to the distaff and spindle, spinning all of the baskets of wool into fine thread. The coarser thread she would use to weave cloth, while the fine thread would be reserved for embroidery. Though she tried to keep her mind occupied the Norsemen was never far from her thoughts.

She wondered how Bjorn's wound was healing. Was he on the mend or had the wound putrefied? Why had he not sent for her?

"Mathilda, how fares the Viking chief?" She couldn't bring herself to speak his name.

"Milord seems well enough," Mathilda answered. "He tends to his business."

"What kind of business?" Gwened asked. "How *does* he spend his days?"

"He rides out each morn through his men's encampment. He meets with the captains and then inspects the crops or rides onward to the village. He speaks much with the farmers and merchants."

Gwened snorted. "No doubt demanding a hefty share of the harvest and profits from the merchants."

"No more than Duke Rudalt took," Mathilda answered. "On the contrary, this one seems more intent on learning how we do things. He even speaks of planting more fields and improving trade with Neustria."

The information took Gwened very much by surprise. As duke, her brother had delegated most of his responsibilities to others so that he could do nothing but drink, hunt, and whore. He gave no thought to planting fields or expanding trade. He cared only for his own pleasures.

"Does he? And what do his men do?" Gwened asked.

"Many of them have taken up the plow, milady."

"They have?"

Gwened took it all in with cynicism. Why would Bjorn and his brothers act with such uncharacteristic restraint? Could it be true that they wanted to settle peacefully in Brittany? She found it hard to believe.

Although her father had finally freed Brittany of the terror, Vikings were still a plague all over Europe. They came every spring and left a path of death and destruction in their wake.

"Do you think this is just a charade, or do you believe they truly wish to become farmers and tradesmen?" Gwened asked. "How long will it be before they experience the overwhelming urge to return to raiding?"

"I think only time will tell, milady," Mathilda said.

And time was passing all too slowly for Gwened. A fortnight had passed with no word from anyone. She coiled the last skein of spun wool with a sigh. "Mathilda, would you please bring me the chamber pots when you collect them each morn?"

Mathilda regarded her with a questioning look. "Whatever for, milady?"

"I need the urine to extract the dye from the lichens I collected."

"Milady, the Norsemen do not use the chamber pots."

"They don't?"

"Nay." Mathilda shook her head.

"My men prefer to relieve themselves out of doors,"

answered a deep voice. Gwened looked up to find Bjorn standing in the doorway. He regarded her with a strangely hostile look. "You have not left this room for two days."

"I have been busy," she replied, nodding to the baskets.

"*You* spun all of this?"

"Aye," Gwened answered. "I have spun it and now I intend to dye it. I don't know why this should surprise you. My mother was a queen, yet she spun her own thread. Are Norse women not encouraged to be industrious?"

"They are very industrious," he replied.

"Why have you come here?" she asked.

"The wound is red and hot," he said. "It pains me."

"Then why are you walking about?"

"Because you did not come to me," he answered with a glower.

"You did not ask me to."

"I didn't *want* to ask," he muttered.

Gwened shook her head with a sigh. Did all men consider it a weakness to seek help? Or was it just women they refused to be indebted to?

"You will look at it?" he asked.

"Aye. Come." She beckoned him to follow her into the adjoining bedchamber.

Gwened's skin prickled the moment he entered the room behind her. The queen's bedchamber was spacious and well-lit, with sun shining through the large windows, but suddenly felt small and airless in his presence. Why was it so difficult to breathe when he was near?

"You need to remove your trews," she said, spinning her back as he proceeded to undress.

"Should I remain standing or should I sit?" he asked.

"'Twould be best if you lie on the bed," she answered, waiting as the mattress groaned under his weight.

"I am ready."

Gwened turned to discover him lying naked from the waist down, but at least this time his shirt covered his privates. He was grinning at her.

"What is so funny?" she snapped.

"You," he replied. "Why are you so afraid of me? To my friends, I am quite harmless."

"We are not friends," she replied.

His brow cocked. "You would refuse friendship to

one who saved your life? 'Tis not the way of it where I come from."

"I *owe* you my gratitude," she said, "but friendship cannot be based on obligation, it must be freely given."

"What if I asked for your friendship? Would you still deny me?"

She licked her lips and considered his question. "I would wonder *why* you ask," she replied. "Friendship between a man and a woman is not a common thing." She knelt beside him and drew his shirt up. His flesh was hot under her fingers and the skin was an angry shade of red. "It does not look well. Did you apply the poultice?"

"Aye," he answered, "but I ran out."

"Why didn't you tell me?"

"I thought you would come."

His eyes flickered with an emotion she couldn't quite decipher. Was he actually *hurt* that she hadn't checked on him? For the first time, she noticed the brightness of his eyes and the pink tinge to his cheeks. "Are you feverish?"

"Perhaps," he confessed with a shrug.

"'Tis good you sought me," she said. "Mathilda!" she called out. "Pray bring me hot water, yarrow, and honey!"

"Aye, milady," her maid replied.

Gwened then rose to retrieve her own wash basin and a clean cloth. As she cleansed his wound, she suddenly realized this might be her chance to escape. If he became feverish, he would be unable to pursue her. She only needed to drug him with mandragora. He would sleep deeply, and no one would be the wiser. She could then return home.

But even as she formulated the plan, she knew she could not go through with it. He had indeed saved her life, and she was indebted to him for that reason, if nothing else. But there *was* something else. Something she'd tried to ignore—his trust. He had come to her, *trusting* her to heal him. Perhaps she was a fool for not seizing the opportunity, but enemy or not, she couldn't betray the faith that he'd placed in her.

Suddenly she understood Adèle's actions. Ironically, she found herself in a very similar position—forced to choose between fighting or helping the enemy. Like Adèle, Gwened had been left with no defenses, but neither of these Norsemen seemed inclined to abuse their power.

When Mathilda returned with the herbs, Gwened

mixed part of the yarrow in a cup of hot water as a fever tea, then added a generous dose of mandragora to help the pain, with some honey to combat the bitter taste. She saved the rest of the herbs and honey to make another poultice.

"Drink this," she commanded, handing him the cup.

His golden gaze sought hers. "What is in it?"

"Yarrow and mandragora. 'Tis good to treat fever."

"Mandragora? Is that what made me dream?"

"It has been known to induce vivid dreams," she said.

"Do you intend to drug me and escape?"

"I was thinking of it," she confessed.

"'Twould do no good. My men would catch you."

"Why do you keep me here? What do you want from me?"

"Your goodwill… Peace in Poher."

"Ah! Poher," she replied. "That is the real reason you hold me! You fear a rebellion against your wounded brother. How badly was he hurt?"

"I hate to disappoint you, but my brother, thank the gods, is on the mend. I expect his return very soon."

"And then what?" she asked.

"I will accompany you back to your home."

"There is no need. I have my men to escort me."

"You misunderstand, Countess. I do not go as your escort. I go in my brother's service. I will remain in Poher to administer his affairs. And I expect your cooperation."

"My cooperation? I won't give it to you and I won't give up Poher!"

"I don't *ask* for it. You have no choice in that matter. I only *ask* that you care for my wounds."

Gwened was at first tempted to throw the bowl of poultice in his face, but she somehow managed self-restraint. She wasn't particularly gentle in applying it this time, but other than a grunt or two, the Viking made no complaint.

When Bjorn opened his eyes, the room was dark, save for a flickering rushlight. He sat up in confusion. This wasn't his bed or his chamber. Where was he?

"How do you feel?"

It took a moment before the countess' face came fully into focus. "What in Odin's name did you put in that tea?" he groaned. "My head feels as if I've been struck by Thor's hammer."

"I added some poppy extract to help you sleep. It seems to have worked."

"Too well," he grumbled. "How long have I been unconscious?"

"A day and a half," she answered. "It appears your fever has finally broken. How is your leg?"

He reached down to touch the flesh. The heat and pain had dissipated. "It seems improved."

"Good," she said. "I would very much like to have my bed back."

"It is a large bed," he commented with a grin, "there is room for two."

"I am accustomed to sleeping alone," she replied stiffly.

Her answer was all too telling. "Your husband does not sleep with you? Is that why you are childless?"

She stared back at him wide-eyed. "How would you know I am childless?"

"'Tis obvious. You never voiced concern over the care of your children when I said I would keep you here. Any mother would have done so. Are you barren?"

Her face flushed. "I don't have any reason to believe I am, but Mateudoi has not been a true husband to me. Ours was not a... normal... marriage."

"He prefers men?"

"No!" Gwened exclaimed aghast. "At least I have no reason to believe such a thing."

"Then he must have a mistress."

"Mateudoi's only mistress is the Holy Mother Church!" she declared bitterly.

Her answer confused him. "I have not heard these things of the Christians. They condemn our fertility rites, yet perform sexual acts with the priestess of your church?"

"There is no priestess!" she declared with a look of exasperation. "I didn't mean a literal mistress. I meant that his devotion is only to the Church. Before we wed, he was studying for the priesthood. He never wanted the marriage... he never wanted me."

Bjorn studied her with growing incredulity. What sane man would reject such a woman? "I cannot comprehend this. Why would he not desire you?"

"Because Mateudoi is not like other men... he is malformed."

"Aye? What is the nature of this deformity?" he

asked.

"The left side of his body is crippled," she replied. "He has difficulty walking and has limited use of his left hand, but he is otherwise whole."

Bjorn snorted. "Your family forced you to wed such a man? In my country, he would have been given back to the gods at birth."

"You mean left to die? His father wanted to do that, but his mother did not."

"She disobeyed her husband?"

"She protected her child! Any loving mother would do the same."

"Would you have nurtured such a child?" he asked. "You would have allowed it to suffer?"

"Mateudoi does not suffer," she said. "True, he does have some physical limitations, but he is a brilliant scholar."

"Do you know so little of men?" he scoffed. "Do you really think he would have *chosen* to live this way had he been allowed to choose?"

"I don't know his mind on the matter," she said softly. "I don't really know him at all."

"So you are married to a cripple who cannot protect you, provide for you or even sire children upon you. This makes no sense! Why do you continue in this farce of a marriage? Why not divorce him? A Norse woman would not hesitate to do so."

"There is no divorce. Our Church is very strict about marital unions. A marriage can only be dissolved by a special dispensation from the Pope. It can take months or even years... if it is granted at all."

"It is a husband's duty to give his wife children," he declared. "Do you not desire them?"

"Yes," she answered sadly. "I do."

"Then the solution is simple. If you cannot divorce him—take a lover."

Her eyes flickered. "'Tis not done! 'Twould be adultery."

He shook his head with a humorless laugh. "Though I try, I cannot comprehend your nonsensical Christian beliefs."

"Nor can I comprehend your animal sacrifices," she challenged.

"My gods require gifts for special favors. Have you never offered anything to your god in exchange for something you desire?"

"I offer my prayers, my obedience, and my devotion. My God does not require any other sacrifice. Why do you feel compelled to offer *every* boar you kill? Is one not enough?"

"It can take many offerings to remove a curse," he replied.

Her gaze softened. "Why would you believe you are cursed?"

"Because one moment I had everything and the next I had nothing! The gods took my wife and child from me."

"I lost Hugo," she said softly. "But I do not blame God." She was silent for a long moment. "At least that's what I tell myself."

"Yet you also feel cursed?"

"Perhaps. How can I not when my whole world is crumbling?" she replied with a bitter laugh. "I have no husband, no children, my brother is dead, and now Vikings have invaded my homeland."

Her desolate expression moved him. He reached for her hand. "You are a beautiful woman, Gwened. You could have any man you desired."

She shook her head. "I have never known that kind of desire for a man."

"What of this Hugo? You said you loved him."

"I did love him," she said. "Everyone loved him.

But we were never together that way. We merely exchanged a few kisses. We were chaste."

"*Chaste*?" Bjorn nearly roared with laughter. "He did not lie with you? A man loves a woman with his body or he does not love her at all!"

"I don't believe that!" she snapped.

"You would if you had ever experienced it."

"Get out!" she cried. She jerked the covers off the bed "Get out of my bed and out of my chamber!"

"The truth offends you?"

"*You* offend me!" She answered with a shove that nearly sent him tumbling to the floor.

Her eyes flashed with fury. He would never have imagined the icy countess a woman of such strong passion. He also never could have imagined becoming aroused by it…but he was.

Undeniably aroused.

He reached for her.

She slapped at his arms and pounded his chest as he pulled her into an embrace, but he wasn't the true cause of her fury. It was pain she unleashed. Raw and unadulterated. He recognized it because he had lived it.

Though she continued to fight, her protests grew weaker until she finally buried her face against his chest and sobbed.

>>><<<

GWENED WEPT UNTIL she could weep no more while Bjorn held her close, enveloping her in his strong arms and in his musky scent. She was furious that he'd pushed her to her breaking point, but at the same time, she was strangely relieved to have unburdened the secrets of her heart.

"Are you finished now?" His rumbled out of the chest that lay against her ear.

"I'm finished." Yet, she couldn't seem to break away from him.

It felt good to be held. Why did she feel safe in her enemy's embrace? She couldn't comprehend it, nor could she deny it. Until this moment, Gwened hadn't realized just how deeply she'd craved a man's touch. For the past six years, she'd been living a half-life. Devoid of love and joy, she felt as if she were slowly withering away.

Bjorn had given her the touch she desperately needed, but it was more than just warmth and comfort. Beneath the surface, something else was growing. An acute awareness of his body made her tingle deep inside. As he slightly shifted his stance, she realized he felt it, too. He was aroused.

His arms loosened but he didn't release her. Instead, he tilted her face upward. His eyes dropped down to her mouth. "I want you," he said in a husky voice. "And I have denied myself for a long time. If you still want me to go. Tell me *now*."

Gwened knew what she *should* say, but somehow the words evaded her.

"Countess," he repeated. "Do you want me to go?"

"Gwened," she said. "My Christian name is Gwened. I give you use of it."

"Gwened, do you understand what will happen if I stay?"

She dumbly nodded her head.

It wasn't a question. It was an inevitability.

What was she doing? Only moments ago, she'd rejected his suggestion that she take a lover. She knew it was morally wrong, but she ached with loneliness. She had been denied so much in life. If she couldn't have love, why couldn't she at least know passion? Just this one time?

"Do you intend only to take your own pleasure?" she asked.

"You wonder what is in it for you?" He moved in closer, close enough that she felt the heat of his body. Her breathing quickened as he cupped her buttocks and pressed himself against her. Her insides jolted with a strange and wonderful sensation as her intimate parts made contact with his.

She licked her lips, her pulse racing with nervous anticipation. "You will make it pleasurable for me also?"

The corner of his mouth twitched. "I am certain you don't know what you ask for, but I assure you I am more than happy to oblige."

Her instincts told her that he would be nothing like her Mateudoi. She wanted this. She wanted *him*.

"Then stay." Though her body trembled, she willed steadiness to her voice. "As you observed earlier, the bed is big enough for two."

CHAPTER ELEVEN

Even as he sat on the mattress, Bjorn still struggled with guilt. He told himself that they were only two people meeting each other's physical needs, that there was nothing more between them. She desired a night of passion and he intended to give it to her. After that, they would be done. No words of love, no talk of the future.

He reached out and drew her between his knees. "You have naught to fear."

"I do not fear," she replied, yet her hands trembled as she fumbled with the laces at the back of her dress.

"Turn around," he commanded, making quick work of loosening her kirtle. Her body quivered as he raised the garment over her head. The light was dim but her thin shift hid little from him as he took in the outline of her feminine body.

He loosened the strings at her neck and the shift slipped from her shoulders. It slid down her body and landed in a whisper at her feet. Slowly and appreciatively, he looked his fill. She was slender with long shapely legs and smooth white skin. Her breasts were small but well-shaped with erect nipples that le longed to suckle.

His gaze dipped to the shadowy place between her thighs. His gaze lingered on the crux of her womanhood. His mouth watered for a taste. She wanted to know pleasure, and he fully intended to give it to her.

She shivered.

"Are you cold, or do you tremble because I am looking at you?" he asked.

"'Tis the *way* you look. You remind me of a wolf," she said.

Her answer made him chuckle. He felt like one, untamed and hungry. "Is that why you have the look of a frightened sheep?"

She drew back arms wrapped protectively over her breasts. "If I displease you, there is no need to take this any further."

Bjorn stifled a groan. He was not accustomed to conversation during sex. He also wasn't accustomed to timid, inexperienced women. But she obviously needed reassurance, and his raging erection needed relief.

"I find you very pleasing. Come, Gwened," he softly urged. "Let me show you. Let me touch you."

She licked her lips and took a cautious step toward him.

He reached out and stroked the backs of his fingers over her cheek, along her neck, and then down to one milky white breast. He stroked a beaded nipple with his thumb, and she shivered again. Her sweet scent tantalized him and her breath felt warm against his face. She tilted her head back, silently telling him she wanted more. It pleased him that she didn't pull away.

He pressed his mouth to the skin of her neck and worked his way down her shoulders to her beckoning breasts. He lavished them with hot, kisses, rooting from one breast to the other. He then suckled her nipples until she clutched her fingers in his hair and whimpered. Her passionate response fired his hunger for her.

He drew her onto the bed and worked his way down her body, skirting his mouth over her smooth belly, while his hands caressed her long, sleek thighs. The scent of her arousal was growing stronger, teasing and tormenting him. His gently probing fingers were rewarded with a warm wetness that nearly blinded him with lust.

It was agony knowing she was ready, but he'd made her a promise that he had every intention of keeping.

※

THOUGH SHE'D DENIED it, Gwened was indeed afraid. But it wasn't Bjorn that evoked her fear, it was the reactions of her body to his. The sensations overwhelmed her. She could never have imagined experiencing such bliss from a man's touch, but when he'd suckled her breasts, she thought she would die. His mouth was like fire on her flesh, searing every inch of her as he moved down her body.

"You are ready for me," he rumbled.

"What do you *mean* ready?"

"This," he remarked, probing a finger into the dampness that pooled between her thighs. "You are very wet."

She squirmed in embarrassment, but he seemed pleased rather than repulsed by it.

"Do not be ashamed." He pressed his hands against her thighs, gently pushing them apart. "I want to look upon you. I want to kiss you."

Gwened gasped. "You can't mean there? Surely that

is wickedness!"

"Wickedness?" He laughed. "Pleasure is the greatest gift the gods ever gave us. There are many means beyond copulation to achieve release. If I am willing to share this gift, why would you reject it?"

He rubbed his soft beard against her inner thighs. His breath was hot and moist as he began kissing, then licking. His mouth was merciless as he teased and tortured her with his tongue, until nothing existed beyond his mouth and her body.

As the sensations continued to swell, Gwened shut her eyes on a whimper. It was too much. Just as she thought she could take no more, something burst inside her, seizing her mind and body with endless echoes of ecstasy.

※

BJORN'S BOLLOCKS THROBBED for release as he'd watched her climax, but having now kept his promise, he would deny himself no longer. Just as he came over her, poised to finally empty his aching bollocks, her body stiffened, as if expecting a violent assault.

Odin's eye! He'd given her pleasure. What was she afraid of? Bjorn threw himself onto his back with a groan.

"What is wrong?" she whispered.

"I've never taken an unwilling woman."

"I told you I wanted this."

He rolled onto his side to face her. "Your body says otherwise."

"I have little experience and you are a very large man. How can you blame me? Please, can we try again?"

Sensing her need for reassurance, he pulled her to him. His gaze dropped to her mouth. Kissing her had never been part of his plan...at least not on her lips. But kissing would surely soothe her anxiety. He cupped her face and plied his lips to hers.

It was only a kiss, but the moment he tasted her, everything changed. Perhaps it was the look of wonderment in her eyes as she surrendered her mouth or the way she molded her body to his. Whatever it was filled him with an overwhelming sense of rightness.

Testing the boundaries of this new sensation, he deepened his exploration. Their breaths mingled as she yielded to his seeking tongue. The kiss continued to intensify, mimicking the motions of thrust and retreat. The ache in his loins returned with a vengeance. He'd never experienced so much power in a kiss.

He was in agony to be inside her.

He rolled her beneath him, never breaking the kiss. Moaning and clinging, she opened her body to him. She tensed only for a moment as he gripped her hips and plunged into welcoming wetness. Though the restraint almost killed him, he held himself back, allowing her to adjust to the fullness before he began moving.

He urged her legs upward and wrapped them tightly around his flanks as he settled into a slow rhythm of plunge and drag. Her soft sighs soon mingled with his guttural groans, her inner walls squeezing him as she began meeting his strokes.

Squeezing his eyes shut, he thrust deeper, harder, faster. His bollocks tightened in his urgent race to release. Suddenly his world contracted, exploding in a burst of heat and light that left him utterly dazed and sated.

※※※

GWENED AWOKE TO the warmth of morning light streaming through the window, but it was nothing compared to the glow she felt within. She was a changed woman. It was as if she'd been liberated from a lifetime of bondage, obligation, and guilt. She would never view the world through the same eyes.

Bjorn was still soundly asleep, his light snores rumbling from deep within his chest. He lay with his head turned toward her. His nose was strong and proud with a small hump at the bridge. Had he broken it? His square jaw was lightly bearded. She shivered at the recollection of his bristle against her skin.

Her gaze lingered on his mouth and the soft, full lips that had filled her with indescribable delight. She flushed at the remembrance of the lavish attention he'd paid to her most intimate places, but it was the kiss on her lips she remembered best. The moment their lips met, everything had changed. Finally, she understood the potency of sexual desire. It was a truly formidable force.

They had become lovers in truth, yet she wasn't fool enough to think herself in love. Love was built on mutual trust, respect, and devotion—none of which they shared, but they had indeed shared an undeniable passion.

Tingling commenced deep in her belly she studied the corded muscle of his forearm and the light dusting of hair that disappeared as her gaze tracked up his bulging bicep to his broad shoulders. The sheet was wrapped around one leg, leaving the other exposed all the way to his well-developed buttocks. The night before, she'd clutched those firm globes of muscle as he'd thrust into her. She suddenly felt a deep urge to feel him again.

As if reading her mind, he rolled onto his side and pulled her against his body. His eyes never opened as he nuzzled her neck and mumbled an incomprehensible string of Norse into her ear. He reached a hand between her thighs and prodded her from behind. Her breath hitched. Was this yet another form of pleasure he'd spoken of? Thinking only of the child she desperately craved, Gwened allowed him to do as he pleased. To her delight, he pleased *her* as well.

Hours later, when she once more opened her eyes… he was gone. Yet, the remnants of their lovemaking remained, the stickiness of his seed still clung to her inner thighs and his musk scented the linens. It was an earthy, pungent scent that stirred her insides.

She wondered if his seed had taken root. Surely such a big and virile man would sire a strong child. The thought secretly thrilled her. Instinctively, she squeezed her legs together hoping to retain every drop he had spent.

CHAPTER TWELVE

CAREFUL NOT TO wake her, Bjorn crept silently out of Gwened's chamber after passing the entire night as well as a goodly part of the morn in the countess' bed. His body was sated but his mind was clouded. He still loved Astrid but couldn't deny his growing feelings for Gwened. Though he wrestled with guilt, he could not regret his actions. His failure to reconcile his emotions put him in a foul mood.

He needed some distance from this place... from her... to clear his head. He took up a boar spear with the intention of hunting when his captain met him in the bailey.

"I have been looking for you," Lars said.

"And now you have found me. What is it?" Bjorn growled.

"An army approaches!"

"How many?"

"At least a hundred."

"Could it be Valdrik?" Bjorn asked.

"I can't be certain," Lars answered. "They are still too far away."

"Then I will discover for myself," Bjorn said. "Saddle my horse."

A few minutes later, Bjorn was galloping toward the advancing war party. It wasn't long before he identified his brother. He spurred his horse onward.

Valdrik followed suit.

They met up with a joyful shout.

"Bjorn!" Valdrik swung down from his saddle.

Bjorn did the same and they came together in a bone-crushing embrace.

"I am glad to see you looking so well, brother," Bjorn said. With his duchess by his side, Valdrik appeared whole, hale, and happy.

"I am well enough to take on any man, but mayhap not an army," Valdrik replied.

"You fear rebellion brewing?" Bjorn asked.

"Ivar has already quashed one in the south, led by Count Ebles of Poitou, but Mateudoi of Poher may be seeking an alliance with Robert of Neustria."

"Why would you think so?" Bjorn asked.

"Because my scouts inform me that the count is

gone from Poher."

"Yet, the countess arrived here over a sennight ago."

"Gwened is *here*?" The duchess remarked with a look of surprise. "Why has she come?"

"'Tis a good question indeed," Bjorn said, his hackles rising with suspicion. Had he been right from the beginning to suspect her motives? Had she only come to distract him while Mateudoi negotiated with the Neustrians? Was seduction part of her plan all along?

"I must go to her at once!" the duchess said. She turned to Valdrik with a swift kiss on the lips. "Pray join me anon, my love."

Bjorn witnessed the exchange with a mixture of envy and resentment. Their affection for one another was surely genuine. He'd had experienced such a thing once before and had secretly begun to hope that he might know it again. But it seemed Gwened had only used him.

Valdrik's arrival had burned away the haze that had muddled his mind. With emotions back in check, he was once more thinking clearly.

"I need you to go to Poher before Mateudoi can organize any resistance against us."

"What of *her*?" Bjorn said, unable to utter the betrayer's name.

"The countess? Take her with you. She will be a stabilizing influence."

Bjorn snorted. "I wouldn't be too sure of that! I doubt she can be trusted."

"Then I will depend upon *you* to manage her," Valdrik said.

Bjorn mumbled a curse. He resigned himself to do as his brother expected…but he didn't like it. He was painfully aware of how well *she* had managed *him*.

"And what of her husband, Mateudoi? What would you have me do with him?"

"Mateudoi is weak and feeble," Valdrik said. "He will be no trouble as long as he does not get aid from the Neustrians. You must ensure that does not happen."

"How?" Bjorn asked. "Would you have me kill him?"

Valdrik cocked his brow. "I leave the matter for you to decide."

※※※

GWENED WAS HAPPILY spinning wool when Adèle

entered the solar.

"Adèle?" Gwened rose with a smile and extended her arms to her sister-in-law. "I am overjoyed to see you!"

"And I, you!" Adèle replied, hugging her back. "I was surprised to hear you had come to Vannes."

"I came as soon as I heard about the invasion," Gwened said. "You can imagine my distress when you were not here. Are you well, sister?"

"I am indeed," Adèle answered. "I assume you know what happened here?"

"Aye," Gwened replied grimly. "I never thought you would concede Brittany so easily!"

"What choice did I have? Rudalt left me alone with no defenses!"

"I am sorry for Brittany," Gwened said.

"I feel much as you do, but I cannot mourn the duke," Adèle said. "I would never have wished this conquest of our lands, but all is not as dire as it seems. There is still much you do not know."

Though Adèle seemed to want to reassure her, Gwened was still dubious. "What happened in Quimper?"

"Quimper has fallen," Adèle answered with a sigh.

"Count Gormaleon put up a fight but was killed in battle. Emma continued to rebel but was also subdued after a time. She has now come to an understanding with Valdrik's brother, Ivar. They have agreed to rule Quimper together."

"Emma, too? I can hardly believe it!" Had the Viking men woven some kind of love spell over the Breton women? She strongly feared that she, too, had fallen under their Pagan enchantment.

"Take heart, sister." Adèle laid a hand on her arm. "It is truly not as bad as it seems. Valdrik has proven himself an honorable man "I believe he will make a far better duke than Rudalt."

Gwened was incredulous. "You are *happy* with this Viking? I thought he *forced* you into marriage."

"He did not *exactly* force me, but marriage to him was the better of two evils. I know this will be hard for you to understand but I have come to respect him... I have also come to love him."

"But it is so...so...sudden!" Gwened protested. Even as she protested, she was reminded of her own tender feelings for Bjorn.

"What of you?" Adèle's expression shifted to concern. "Have you been treated well in my absence?"

Gwened fingered the stitching on her sleeve, wondering how much she dared to confide. "I have not been mistreated, but I long to go home."

"How is it that you came here alone? Where is Mateudoi?"

"I don't know," Gwened confessed.

"Then it is true that he is seeking an alliance with the Neustrians?"

"I doubt it," Gwened replied. "In all likelihood, he knows nothing of the invasion."

Adèle looked puzzled. "How can he not know of this?"

"Because he never returned to Poher. I believe he went to Rome to seek an annulment. I don't know if he ever intends to return."

"Perhaps he will stay in Rome," Adèle said. "He always wanted to enter the church. You have had no word from him in all this time?"

"None," Gwened said.

"Then the fate of Poher remains in your hands."

"Aye," Gwened said.

"You should agree to peace with Valdrik," Adèle said. "He will deal fairly with you. You have my promise on it."

Gwened was still amazed at Adèle's turnabout. "I still don't understand how you can trust him. What makes you believe we are better off under these heathens than in an alliance with Neustria?"

"Because Neustrian aid will only come at a price. In the end, they will reap our wealth and take our sons to be their soldiers. We will be Bretons no more. On the other hand, Valdrik and his brothers will not give up an inch of what they have taken. They intend to stay… and they will protect what they have claimed with their lives."

Gwened released a sad sigh. "Then we are well and truly conquered."

"That's where you are wrong," Adèle said. "As women, we have far more influence than you know."

"Why do you think this?" Gwened asked.

Adèle laid a hand on her belly with a sly smile.

Gwened stared in disbelief. "You cannot be saying that you are…"

"With child?" Adèle finished. "I have every reason to believe I am."

"And it is *his*?"

"Irrefutably," Adèle answered. "And Valdrik's child is the future ruler of all Brittany."

Once more, Gwened was tempted to confess her own secret, but held her tongue. Adèle and Valdrik were bound by marriage, but Bjorn had promised her nothing. What had happened between them could never happen again. She needed to go as far away from him as possible.

"If I agree to cooperate, will Valdrik let me go home?"

"Valdrik wants you to return to Poher, but he's sending Bjorn with you."

"Bjorn is going to Poher?" The news filled her with both joy and dread. "For how long?"

"He will stay indefinitely. Valdrik needs a man he can trust to maintain Poher's defense."

Gwened's thoughts kept her awake long into the night. Though she was reluctant to accept it, Adèle was right. The Neustrians were a longtime foe. In the end, any alliance with them would only result in the loss of Brittany's sovereignty. Perhaps it would be better to be ruled by this band of benevolent Vikings than to be swallowed up by Neustria. She had no doubt that Bjorn would protect Poher, but who would protect her heart?

GWENED AND BJORN rode out early the next morning, accompanied by half of Valdrik's men. Gwened hated to enter her home at the head of an invading army, Valdrik insisted upon a show of strength. It would fall upon her shoulders alone to soften the appearance of hostility.

Although they rode side by side, Bjorn was unusually stiff and silent. His behavior, after their shared night of passion, only hurt and confused her. The tension continued to grow with the passing miles.

"What is wrong?" she asked.

"I dislike being taken for a fool?" he replied in an unsettling tone.

"I don't understand you."

"You lied to me. You used me," he said. "You betrayed my trust."

"*Betrayed* you? How can you say such a thing after…after…" She was all too aware of the men who followed. "I don't know what you are talking about!"

"I speak of your husband's mysterious disappearance. Valdrik told me he is negotiating with Neustria."

"How could I know this?" she protested. "I didn't lie to you. He told me he was going to petition the Pope about…about a personal matter."

His golden eyes slowly assessed her. "The timing of his disappearance and your arrival at Vannes is highly suspicious, *Countess*."

She hated that he'd reverted back to her title.

"I didn't lie to you. What I told you before is true," she said. "I came to Vannes because I needed to know if Adèle was safe. I admit that I had also hoped to buy you off with tribute money. But if that plan failed, I needed to know the strength of your numbers in order to defend my home."

"Yet none of this explains your husband's absence. I ask you again, Gwened, where is the Count of Poher? Be truthful with me and I will go easy on you." His gaze narrowed dangerously. "But if you dare to deceive me again, you will know a heathen's wrath."

"I did not deceive you! How many times must I say it?"

His glower deepened. "You still didn't answer my question. *Where* is your husband and what are his intentions?"

Until now, Gwened had withheld the painful truth, but Bjorn already knew about her failed marriage. What point was there in holding back now? She shut her eyes on a sad sigh. "Mateudoi left me to seek an annulment of our marriage."

"An annulment? Why do you only tell me now? How can I know this isn't another lie to take me off my guard?"

"Is that what you think I did?"

"Aye," he responded with a harsh laugh. "And you succeeded all too well with your innocent seduction and dream-inducing love potions."

"*Dream-inducing love potions*?" It was her turn to laugh. "You think I controlled your dreams? Are you mad? I only gave you medicine for pain!"

He said nothing more.

A moment later, he was no longer riding beside her.

※

OVER THE NEXT two days, Bjorn pushed the pace to Poher, which made it easy to keep his distance from Gwened. He rode in front and put her in the middle of his men which made conversation impossible. In the evenings, when they set up camp, he posted sentries outside her tent. It seemed he was taking no chances.

It was only in the last few miles of the journey that he even allowed her to join him at the front. They hadn't spoken since the day they left Vannes. If he had his way, they wouldn't ever speak again, but there was no avoiding her once they reached their destination. His new position in Poher would require her cooperation.

They arrived at Poher to find the gates closed and archers poised on the ramparts.

"Tell them to raise the portcullis," Bjorn demanded.

"They fear your army," Gwened replied. "Can you blame them?"

"Then go forth and tell them we are no threat," Bjorn demanded.

"Very well," she replied stiffly. Urging her horse forward, Gwened addressed the gatekeeper of Poher. "These men come in peace. Open the gates."

"Milord commanded me otherwise, milady," the gatekeeper replied.

"Milord?" Gwened could barely contain her surprise. "Are you saying Mateudoi has returned?" What could this mean?

"Aye, the count is here," he replied.

"Then go and tell him, 'tis me who desires entrance," she commanded.

Gwened returned to Bjorn. "Mateudoi is within. Please let me go alone to speak with him. He will not trust you."

"And what makes you think *I* trust *you*?" he replied in a tone as cold as the northern seas.

"What has happened? You treat me as if we never…" She looked away.

"As if we never *fucked*?" he finished in a mocking tone.

His answer felt like a knife to her heart. "Is that how you think of it? Is that all it meant to you?"

His full lips curled in contempt. "Why would you ever have thought otherwise?"

Her gaze snapped upward in confusion and fury. She wanted nothing more than to slap the smirk from his handsome face. Was this even the same man with whom she had shared a bed? All of a sudden, he was a stranger. While she hadn't mistaken their passion for love, she had at least believed they'd established trust and friendship. How could she have been so wrong?

"Go," he commanded. "Just know this Countess, if you do not return promptly to open the gate for me, I will not hesitate to set the castle ablaze."

Although the keep was a tower of stone, all of the

other structures within the bailey were made of wood and thatch. It would take little to utterly destroy them.

Gwened knew she had no choice but to do as Adèle had done in Vannes and take on the role of peacemaker. Even if Mateudoi chose to fight Poher lacked the men and resources to withstand a siege. She just hoped that Mateudoi could be convinced to believe her.

"What have you done?" Mateudoi angrily demanded. "Our kingdom is invaded by Vikings and you abandon Poher?"

Gwened responded with a furious laugh. "You abandoned *me*! You left with little explanation and sent no word when you would return!"

"I was on my way to Rome when I learned about the Vikings," he said. "I then abandoned my personal quest to instead request aid from the Marquis of Neustria."

"Why would you seek help from an enemy?" she asked.

"Because we both have the same desire—to drive out these Norsemen," Mateudoi replied.

"Did the marquis agree to this alliance?" she asked.

He nodded. "If we fight the Vikings, they will join us."

"But we cannot fight them!" Gwened said. "Rudalt is dead! Gormaelon of Cornouailles is dead! And we have too few men and no one to lead them!"

He stared at her with a look of incomprehension. "You would just give up? You would sacrifice our land to these godless, murdering savages?"

"To my knowledge, they have committed no murder," Gwened replied. "They fought only those who resisted. If we do not resist, there will be neither bloodshed nor enslavement."

"How can you believe this?" Mateudoi asked.

"Because I have seen it with my own eyes. I went to Vannes. I saw no violence there. Even while I was held hostage I was never mistreated."

"Do you care nothing about the Church?" he asked. "These heathens have desecrated our monasteries! It is an affront to God if we allow them to stay."

"Perhaps in time we can convert them?"

"I cannot take the chance that they will corrupt our own people and lead them into apostasy!"

"At least talk with them," Gwened urged. "What choice have you when their army stands at the gate?"

"One way or another, I will fight them," Mateudoi vowed. Limping toward her, he placed his hands on her shoulders. "But I cannot do it alone. I *need* your support, Gwened." He eyes sought hers. "Do I have it?"

Mateudoi surprised her with his show of strength but his concern was only for the church. Never for her. He cared nothing about her needs.

She suddenly recalled their last night together when she had offered herself in the vain hope that they might have some semblance of a normal life together. In their six years of marriage, she had asked only one this one thing of him and he had heartlessly rebuffed her.

She responded with a bitter laugh. "You want my support?" She then flung his own earlier words back at him. "I'm sorry Mateudoi, you ask for what I cannot give you."

CHAPTER THIRTEEN

DAYS PASSED AT Poher in a tension-filled truce. Sullen and silent, Mateudoi barely left his study, while Gwened retreated to her own haven in hope of avoiding Bjorn. Thankfully, he made it easy by spending as little time as possible in the castle. As his brother's emissary, he spent his days in Poher much as he had done in Vannes.

The three brothers had indeed succeeded in conquering the kingdom, an event that would forever change the fate of Brittany. Suddenly the tapestry she had spent six years on, had new meaning. With needle and woolen thread, Gwened began to record the turn of events. Reaching for a stick of chalk, she began sketching.

Working feverishly, she depicted an army of mounted Vikings, the hand-to-hand combat that killed Duke Rudalt, the wedding of the Viking chief to the widowed duchess, and then the violent assault on

Quimper.

Her thoughts soon turned to Bjorn and her fingers followed.

After a time, she stared down at a rough outline of a Viking battling a boar. That day had marked a turning point in their relationship. At first she had been horrified by his Pagan sacrifice, but now she understood that it wasn't so much an act of bloodlust, but one of contrition.

Once she was satisfied with the sketch, she searched her supply of wool for a particular shade of blue. She had just begun embroidering his tunic when Bjorn entered her solar.

"You invade where you are not wanted," she replied icily. "This is my private place. Please leave."

Ignoring her request, he knelt and took up a section of cloth. "What is this?" His gaze was wide with amazement as he took in the yards of embroidered cloth that stretched the length of the chamber.

"I told you before that I enjoy needlework," she replied matter-of-factly.

"This is not mere needlework!" His brows pulled together as he studied the colorful pictures. "You are a storyteller, Gwened?"

"'Tis my family history, wrought with wool," she replied politely.

"'Tis genius! I have never beheld such artistry!"

"I am gratified by your admiration," she replied, ignoring the warm flush induced by his praise.

He rose and came to her then. "Tell me about this. I would know more. What compelled you to do it?"

"I wanted to ensure that the history of our kingdom would never be forgotten. Although the Church records everything, most of our people are illiterate. Pictures, however, are understood by all."

He gazed down at her tambour and the sketch she had just completed of him battling the boar. Gwened fought the urge to snatch it from view.

"'Tis a good likeness," he remarked. "But perhaps you could make me bigger?" he added with a grin.

"I will not humor your vanity with this," she replied. "Besides, you are already one of the largest men I have ever seen."

"You created this shade of blue?" he asked with a look of admiration. "'Tis even deeper than my tunic."

"I had to experiment, but I am satisfied with the result." She took up her needle and resumed her work, but to her dismay, he still didn't leave.

"Why are you still here?" she demanded.

"Mateudoi told me of your refusal to join in an alliance with Neustria."

"I saw little point in it," she said. "Twould only result in needless death, and Brittany would be no better off under Neustrian control than under yours."

"I am gratified by your good faith," he replied.

"'Tis not so much my faith, as the simple facts," she answered. "Neustria is no friend to Brittany." She stabbed the linen and pulled the thread through it.

He unexpectedly laid his hand on hers. "Please, Gwened. I came to make peace with you. Can there be an end to this enmity between us?"

"We already have peace. I bear you no malice," she said.

"No malice?" he shook his head with a scoffing sound. "Then what we have is nothing more than a truce between foes. 'Tis not enough."

"Not enough?" She snatched her hand away. "What do you want from me? Why do you suddenly come back to me with sweet words? If your bed is too cold, surely there are servants willing to warm it for you."

He stepped back with a sigh. "Why are you making this so difficult?"

Dropping her needle, Gwened stood to face him. "I have given the cooperation you sought. Why do you disturb my peace? Why not just let me be?" she asked in a choked voice.

He gripped her arms in a solid hold. "Maybe because I want more than just your cooperation."

"You once had more," she replied. "But then you acted like a…a…"

"A jackass?" he offered with a look of chagrin.

"Yes!" she hissed. "You are the biggest jackass I ever met."

"Because I thought you betrayed me," he said. "I thought you only came to distract me while Mateudoi worked against us… but now I know this isn't true. Mateudoi told me that you refused to join him in an alliance with Neustria." He cupped her face in his large, warm hand. "I'm sorry I mistrusted you, Gwened. I have guarded myself for a long time."

"As have I," she said. "But there can be nothing between us as long as I am another man's wife."

"What if Mateudoi was out of the way?"

Her throat tightened with fear. "Why would you ask me this? Do you intend to kill him?" She might not love Mateudoi, but she wished him no harm.

"Only as a last resort," Bjorn replied with a smirk. "Happily for him, he wishes to renounce his title and leave Poher."

"And you would let him do this?" she asked.

"I would allow it… if you give me a reason."

"A reason?" Her traitorous heart skipped as she gazed up into his golden-flecked eyes. She hated that she still reacted so strongly to him. "What do you mean?"

"If your husband has chosen to become a priest, your church can have no reason to deny an annulment. Are not priests required to live in abstinence?"

"They are," she said.

"Then I ask if you will have a savage Viking as your husband."

She was growing too flustered to think clearly. "Even if I wanted to marry you annulment proceedings could take some time."

His brow lifted. "Even *if* you wanted me?"

"I refuse to be your next conquest, Bjorn. You have taken Poher, but I will not marry you only to solidify your position here."

"Is that what you think I want?"

"Of course I do and I refuse to enter another loveless marriage."

"I have bedded no other women, Gwened. Ever since I lost my wife, I have desired no one but you."

"Desire is not love," she argued. "After the passion fades, there is only emptiness."

"I too, have such a void for a very long time. There is something more you should know. 'Tis something I have shared with no one."

"And what is that?"

"When I was injured, the goddess Frigg came to me in a dream. She told me the wound in my heart would only heal when I met the one destined to be my life mate. I know now that she meant you."

She snorted in disbelief. "Why would you think that?"

He took her hand and brought it to his chest, placing it under his shirt on his warm, bare skin just above his beating heart. Her own heart skipped a beat as she gazed into his earnest golden eyes. "Because I prayed and sacrificed but found no relief until I found you. Your very touch soothes the ache. Does this mean nothing?"

His words unsettled and confused her. She had once surrendered her body to him but now he seemed bent on claiming her heart and soul. "I don't know what to think…I need time…"

"I am a patient man when I want to be, and I want *you* more than I desire lands and power and riches. All of these things would mean nothing if I cannot also have you."

"Do you really mean that?"

"I told you before that a man loves a woman with his body. If my words cannot convince you, perhaps *this* will."

He took her into his arms for a long, deep kiss that made her long for much more than a single night of passion. No. *This* kiss made her yearn for a lifetime of it.

EPILOGUE

Four months later

"I THOUGHT I would find you here," Bjorn entered her solar with his long and easy stride. She was glad to see a smile on his face as he came toward her.

As always, her pulse raced as he bent his head to place a kiss on her lips.

"What has put you in such a good humor?" she asked.

He produced a rolled parchment from the folds of his tunic.

"What is this?"

"I have been given my heart's desire this day. 'Tis notification of your annulment."

Gwened's breath hitched. It was the answer to her own secret prayers. "What does this mean?" she asked, her heart racing with anticipation.

"If you will have a savage Viking as your husband, I will soon make you my bride."

"Sooner is good...given the circumstances." Gwened licked her lips and glanced down at her tambour.

His gaze followed. "What is this new picture, Gwened?" He gently took it from her hands. His pupils widened as he studied the loving work of her needle. "Tis a babe wearing a crown?"

"Aye," she whispered. "'Tis Brittany's king."

"Brittany no longer has a king."

"'Tis not the past that I depict, but the future, when Brittany will once again be ruled by the line of Alain the Great."

He regarded her quizzically. "King Alain was Duke Rudalt's sire, but Rudalt left no heirs."

"King Alain was also *my* father," she reminded him softly.

His dark expression slowly transformed. "You cannot mean?"

"I carry your son, Bjorn. Our babe will be the only grandchild of the last king, and as thus, the rightful heir. *He* will be the next king of Brittany."

He stared back at her in a stone-cold silence that made her heart sink deep into her belly.

"You are not happy?"

"No one must know this child is mine!"

She fought back a choking sob. "Why would you deny your child?"

"'Tis not by choice!" he replied with an anguished look. "You were still married to Mateudoi when it was conceived. The world *must* believe it is his. I will raise him as my own and guard him with my very life, but this must remain our secret. I will not have him tainted by bastardy."

"But Mateudoi will know!" she protested.

"If he does not agree to silence, I will silence him."

She gasped. "You wouldn't!"

"Indeed, I would," he replied darkly. His frown deepened. "There is something even greater at stake."

"And what is that?" she asked.

"Valdrik," he replied. "My brother is the Grand Duke of Brittany. Your child… our child… will eventually pose a threat to his claim. I love my brother and pledged my life to his service."

Gwened's chest tightened. Mateudoi had placed his devotion to God above all else. Would Bjorn also choose his loyalty to his brother? Did she mean so little to him?

"Are you saying you would support your brother

over your own son?"

He knelt beside her and placed his large, warm hand on her belly. "Nay, Gwened. I can no longer uphold my vow to my brother. There is now another to whom I owe an even greater allegiance. Know this— there is *nothing* I will not do to protect you and the child you carry."

THE END

Author's Note

Readers who are familiar with early European history may recognize that many of the characters and events in my Wolves of Brittany books are either true or inspired by actual people and historical events.

Although THE BASTARD OF BRITTANY takes place about one hundred and fifty years before the Norman conquest of England, The Bayeux Tapestry (a fascinating 220-foot-long example of Noman embroidery depicting the event) was very much the inspiration for this particular story.

By the time of the conquest, Brittany was completely under Norman control, and many Breton nobles crossed the channel with Duke William to conquer England.

If you enjoyed this story, please check out my SONS OF SCOTLAND SERIES!